THE LAST DUCHESS

B. McLane-Iles

MINERVA PRESS
MONTREUX   LONDON   WASHINGTON

THE LAST DUCHESS
Copyright © B. McLane-Iles 1996

All Rights Reserved

No part of this book may be reproduced in any form,
by photocopying or by any electronic or mechanical means,
including information storage or retrieval systems,
without permission in writing from both the copyright owner
and the publisher of this book.

ISBN 1 85863 606 X

First Published 1996 by
MINERVA PRESS
195 Knightsbridge
London SW7 1RE

Printed in Great Britain by
Antony Rowe Ltd., Chippenham, Wiltshire

THE LAST DUCHESS

A drama in five Acts; a total of twenty-six scenes, fourteen different settings.

This is the story of Anne of Brittany, Duchess of Brittany, and her struggle to maintain the sovereignty of her land.

Contents

List of Characters (in order of appearance)	vii
Action and Settings	xiii
Prologue	xv

Act One

Scene I	19
Scene II	23
Scene III	28
Scene IV	41
Scene V	56
Scene VI	76

Act Two

Scene I	106
Scene II	123
Scene III	130
Scene IV	140

Act Three

Scene I	146
Scene II	157
Scene III	188

Scene IV	196
Act Four	
Scene I	211
Scene II	223
Scene III	237
Scene IV	245
Scene V	257
Act Five	
Scene I	270
Scene II	284
Scene III	289
Scene IV	298
Scene V	315
Scene VI	331
Scene VII	354
Scene VIII	363
Scene IX	367
Notes	374

List of Characters

(in order of appearance)

Main characters

Geneviève Vernant	Commentator of the play and personal servant of Anne of Brittany. A character who takes on other minor roles throughout the drama.
Louis d'Orléans	Duke d'Orléans, later to become King Louis XII and second husband to Anne of Brittany.
Charles VIII	Son, heir and successor of Louis XI, the 'Spider King'. First husband of Anne of Brittany.
Anne of Brittany	Duchess of Brittany, later becomes the Queen of France, eldest legitimate daughter of Duke François II of Brittany; last Breton duchess and last sovereign ruler of Brittany.

Secondary characters

Louise de Savoie	Duchess of Angoulême (also the Duchess of Savoie); mother of François d'Angoulême (the future king of France and the successor of Louis XII).
Louis XI ('The Spider King')	French king of the fifteenth century, known for his merciless treatment of political enemies; father of Charles, Jeanne and Anne

	de Beaujeu; political enemy of Brittany and of the League of Princes.
Pierre Landais	Treasurer and later Chancellor of Brittany.
Guillaume Chauvin	Chancellor of Brittany throughout first part of reign of Duke François II, falsely accused by Landais of treason against Duke François.
Baron Philippe de Montauban	Counsellor to Duchess Anne of Brittany
Cesare Borgia	Duke of Valentinois, son of Alexander Borgia (Pope Alexander VI), political adversary of Charles VIII and Louis XII.
Pope Alexander VI	Sovereign head of the Vatican City, leader of the united opposition of the Italian City States against France's invasion and conquest of Italy; father of Cesare Valentine Borgia, amongst others.
François of Angoulême	Heir and adopted son of Louis XII, the future French Renaissance king. The future husband of Claude.
Princess Claude	Heir and eldest daughter of Anne of Brittany and Louis XII. The future queen of France and wife of François I.
Princess Jeanne	Second daughter of 'the Spider King' (Louis XI), first wife of Louis d'Orléans

Archduchess Juana (La Loca) of Castile	Hapsburg Archduchess; wife of Philip of Austria, Archduke; daughter and heir of Queen Isabella of Castile and King Ferdinand of Aragon, mother of the future Hapsburg Emperor and King of Spain, Charles V.
Archduke Philip of Austria	Hapsburg Archduke of the former Holy Roman Empire, son and heir of Emperor Maximilian, father of the future Emperor and King of Spain, Charles V.

Minor players

Cardinal George Amboise

Prince d'Orange (third counsellor of King Louis XII)

Pierre Rohan and young Rohan

Breton aristocrats

Marie de Clèves, Duchess d'Orléans (played by the character Geneviève)

Guard to Louis XI

Count Antoine de Chavannes

A Breton lady

A merchant

Marguerite, Duchess of Brittany, wife of François II

Sieur William Hailsham, companion of Louis d'Orléans

Octave, servant of Louis d'Orléans (played by the character Geneviève)

Madame Françoise Dinan, governess of Anne of Brittany, sister of Maréchal Rieux

Isabeau, younger sister of Anne

Gabrielle, Anne's stepsister, daughter of François II and of Antoinette Meignelais

Antoine, Anne's stepbrother, son of François II and of Antoinette Meignelais

Jehan Meschinot, troubadour and poet

Madame Antoinette Meignelais, mistress of François II of Brittany

Young guard

Old palace guard

Other guards of the palace and of the Prince d'Orange's retinue

A cleric

Henry of Lancaster

Servants engaged in the inn

Madeleine, the innkeeper (played by Geneviève)

Jacques, courtier of Louis d'Orléans

A Breton traveller

Alain d'Albret, a Breton aristocrat

Maréchal Rieux

The first magistrate

The second magistrate

A group of magistrates, bishops, priests, aristocrats and merchants (a gathering of the three estates of the Parliament of Brittany)

Three ambassadors of Charles VIII of France

A messenger of King Charles of France

Ten knights in the service of Maréchal Rieux

A merchant and his servant

Gian Galeazzo Sforza, King of Milan

Ludovico Sforza, Regent of Milan

Pietro Medici, prince of Florence

Damsels of Queen Anne's court

Clément Marot, the son of Jean Marot, poet of the Renaissance

Jean Marot, poet of Queen Anne's court

Chambermaid (played by Geneviève)

Yves, a Breton peasant

A young priest

Arrezzo, the Papal Nuncio in Paris, Bishop of Setta
The priest
The messenger

Action and Settings

ACT ONE	Scenes I–III	Interior chamber of sixteenth-century French palace, the Château de Blois
	Scene IV	Nantes, Brittany, marketplace and the courtyard of the Château de Nantes
	Scene V	Court of François II, Duke of Brittany
	Scene VI	Salon of François II
ACT TWO	Scene I	Château de Nantes; courtyard and Duke's parlour
	Scene II	Château de Nantes; salon of François II
	Scene III	An inn to the north of Blois
	Scene IV	Geneviève's chambers in the inn
ACT THREE	Scene I	Nantes, Brittany, before the château
	Scene II	Parliament hall in Rennes
	Scene III	Outside Nantes Château
	Scene IV	Interior hall of Parliament at Rennes
ACT FOUR	Scene I	Rome, interior of Farnese palace
	Scenes II and III	French court at Amboise
	Scene IV	Combined scene of exterior view of French bedchamber in Amboise and royal parlour in Lyon, juxtaposed with elements and characters of papal and Savoy courts.
	Scene V	Court in the Amboise palace of Charles VIII

ACT FIVE	Scene I	Outside Nantes, a small hamlet and large field.
	Scene II	Juxtaposition of elements from scene outside Nantes in field, from scene of Roman papal court and from scene of d'Orléans's court at Blois
	Scene III	Court of King Louis II at Blois
	Scene IV	Outside Nantes, a small hamlet and large field combined with scene of Blois parlour
	Scene V	Bedchamber of Blois Château
	Scene VI	Salon of Blois Château, elegantly furnished
	Scene VII	Courtyard of Blois Château
	Scene VIII	Paris, in front of Notre Dame Cathedral, where a theatrical farce is being presented to Queen Anne
	Scene IX	Court of Blois, château of King Louis XII

Prologue

Prior to the beginning of the play, audience will hear the first few minutes of the late fifteenth-century song 'En amour n'a si non bien' (1). The singer is accompanied by a lute and medieval harp players. The curtain rises two minutes before the song ends. The musicians and singers, unless otherwise indicated in the course of the drama, perform below the stage, unseen by the audience. The scene is an interior chamber of a French palace, the Château de Blois of King Louis XII of France. The date is 1513. Costumes and architecture of the play reflect this period. Geneviève Vernant, a woman in her forties in modest medieval costume, comes out sweeping. Lights fade on the rest of the stage and project slowly on her. Vernant looks up slowly, notices the audience and curtseys apologetically.

GENEVIÈVE VERNANT

Ah, beg pardon. I'll be only a moment.

(She scurries towards stage right, removes her apron and sets it with the broom against the hall. She touches her hair and breathes heavily, sighing from the discomfort of her tight bodice. Arranging herself and smiling in a very satisfied way, Geneviève comes back centre stage towards the audience. Taking a deep breath of surprise and great satisfaction, she resumes speaking.)

Well, indeed, this is a good group tonight – filled completely with ladies and gentlemen. Good evening to you all. I am called Geneviève, Geneviève Vernant. But my name is not essential to the story of Queen Anne, Duchess of Brittany. I am one of the unidentifiable faces of her day. Throughout the drama you will see this evening, I will appear from time to time. But pay that no mind. Well! *(Geneviève eagerly claps her hands.)* Shall we begin? *(Signals for lights to come up and continues in a direct tone.)* My Lady Anne died some months ago, having lived to the ancient age of thirty-seven. Here is her chapel in the Blois palace. I come here often with my children. To us Bretons, Anne might have been a saint for all she did as Duchess of Brittany, consolidating the realm and protecting us against both French and English invasion, preserving the Breton identity. After a terrible war with France in which many of my own family died, our Breton Duchess Lady Anne married two French kings, one right after another. All this, of course, was not complete self-sacrifice. You've got to understand that women in my time, even those of royal blood, had to be practical. But, for a time, it saved Breton sovereignty. Well, I'm chattering on while you're sitting there waiting for the play to begin. Right, we'll be starting with the end and moving back and forth in time, so you must watch carefully. *(As Vernant finishes this sentence a corner of the room lights up showing King Louis XII studying a parchment on a wooden table, surrounded by three counsellors.)* There's Louis XII, Anne's second husband, the King of France, with his counsellors. Louis will be helping me tell you the story.

They're arranging the marriage of Princess Claude to Duke François of Savoy. That's right, you know your history. Anne's heir and treasured daughter, Claude, will die young of smallpox. She will have been neglected and dominated by her husband, François, the glorious king of the French Renaissance. And Brittany crushed and absorbed into the French realm by François d'Angoulême, de Savoie, King of France. Ah, my Lady Anne had battled beyond belief to avoid such a thing. Every time I think of it, my heart starts to pound... Ah, you must excuse me, I've another room to sweep and other roles to play... but first... a most uncomfortable corset to relinquish. *(Exits)*

Short musical presentation of 'Ne dors pas' composed by Guillaume Dufay in 1474 (2).

ACT ONE

SCENE I

Scene takes place in the palace. Louis speaks to his counsellors, including Cardinal Amboise and the Prince d'Orange. Duchess Louise de Savoie is also present.

LOUIS XII

(completing his signature and rolling up a parchment)

The decree is final. Claude will marry the Duke d'Angoulême in three weeks hence. And I shall live to crown my successor.

AMBOISE *(taking the parchment)*

Very good, my lord.

PRINCE D'ORANGE

The queen would not have had it so, Your Majesty. Brittany is henceforth relinquished to the crown. Claude, the would-be Hapsburg Empress and Duchess of Brittany, is no more than François's concubine.

LOUIS XII

That is my daughter of whom you speak, sir. She will be more than that.

DUCHESSE D'ANGOULÊME

And my son, sir, whose promiscuity you imply?

LOUIS XII

It is not implied, madam. It is well established. *(pausing)* But Claude, my progeny, Anne's eldest and sole surviving Catholic heir. . . though neither Brittany's angel of redemption nor Charles

V's empress... the violent relentless dreams of my Lady Anne... though not all this, Claude will be your queen *(taking a silent, long breath)*. And now, I owe homage and repentance to her mother, Anne, Queen of France and Duchess of Brittany, the last Breton duchess indeed. *(Pause.)* What senseless contradiction lived within her... duchess of a proud disappearing race and queen of the conquerors of this vanquished Celtic people.

DUCHESSE D'ANGOULÊME

My lord, she was lost in her dreams. The loss of her children made her insanely ambitious for Claude, and determined to reincarnate her father's defiance of your uncle, Louis XI, when he reigned as king long ago. She opposed until her death your guardianship of my son and his rights to succession.

LOUIS XII

Who, my lady, had greater rights to her dreams – Anne or yourself?

DUCHESSE D'ANGOULÊME

You misunderstand me, sir *(surprised and taken aback)*!

LOUIS XII

Nay, I have never done so, Louise *(looking at her meaningfully)*. But whatever dreams may be whoever's victory, François shall reign as Claude's master and France's King. I need the Duke's succession. The Emperor shall have neither my daughter nor my kingdom. Leave me now – my own marriage approaches.

(Exeunt omnes except Louis XII)

END OF SCENE I

SCENE II

LOUIS XII

Look upon me, Anne. Do I seem robust enough to mate with England's young Mary? Will I survive her passion as I did yours? God knows, your opposition strengthened me in early days of rebellion against the crown, in the months of imprisonment, in the years of service to Charles, my predecessor and your first husband. In those times before I became king, before I lost the privilege of the regional loyalty of the proud Bretons, I held my sword against all who forcibly sought your hand, against all who covetously eyed Brittany, all to whom your father had foolishly promised you. My worthy polygamous fool of a friend, your father, François II, Duke of Brittany. And he *was* my friend *and* my comrade in arms. But he used you, Anne, to buy time and political alliances. The list of your suitors was long, wasn't it? First there was Dunois, my bastard cousin *(lights on stage show Dunois, standing with cape, hat and sword, grey-bearded)*, then Les Rohans *(lights show father and son,* both mature, gleaming, in dark costumes of Breton aristocracy. Lights fade on Les Rohans and on Dunois after a few moments' glimpse). But, most importantly, Maximilian of Austria *(lights show gloriously attired powerful, tall figure)*, Hapsburg Emperor *(lights fade after a few moments)*, and Edward V *(lights on, showing a young boy dressed in Tudor black, drawn, sadly but fatalistically looking upwards towards the shadow of a male figure with a sword)*, your officially recognised child fiancé, who was murdered in the Tower of London, a heinous act historically attributed to his uncle Richard III, but from which Henry of Lancaster and your competitive Breton noble suitors had much to gain. And finally, the King of France, Charles VIII, pushed to conquer Brittany by his calculating sister, Anne de Beaujeu and her husband, Pierre, Duke of Bourbon, both of whom in so doing sought to fulfil the unscrupulous legacy of Louis XI, the former king, my uncle.

(Lights appear, showing Charles VIII, flanked by the Beaujeux. Lights fade again. Louis takes a long deep pause and says in a sad, soft tone)

They all became our enemies, didn't they, my love? *(Suddenly, cynical and practical)* Grudgingly, I must admit that I would have done as Charles had in vanquishing Breton sovereignty, and in the end, finally, that was the course I took. *(Triumphant, yet melancholy)* Which brings us to this moment, Anne – of declaration, of celebration – for, in three weeks hence, as you have heard, Claude, our child will marry, not the Emperor's heirs, but François, Duke of Savoy, my adopted son. France will be safe from the Austrians and François will breathe new life into my heirless, exhausted lineage. But Brittany will be permanently absorbed into the royal domain, no doubt after my death. *(serious yet ironic)* It is for this, my Queen, and for the sacrifice for France of our eldest daughter to an arrogant, ambitious nobleman of unimpeachable sexual prowess. Anne, for the sacrifice of Claude, our child, and Brittany, your homeland. . . *(pause)*, I beg your forgiveness. Humbly, but without regret, for I am no longer Brittany's defender but King of France *(pause of twenty to thirty seconds)*. So still – how could stones and shadows vanquish the passion, life and faith of my Anne! Cruel, indifferent silence, be still while I remember my wife.

(Scene is darkened somewhat as we hear softly the Renaissance melody 'Greensleeves' (3))

LOUIS XII

You were born in mid-winter, Anne, miraculously. Your mother, Marguerite de Foix, second wife to François II, Duke of Brittany, laboured long and silently to bring her husband the long-awaited heir of the nearly extinct Montfort lineage. At last, you began to emerge from your mother's womb into your father's hands. And your life was reflected in the eyes of your father, in his quivering lips as he kissed Marguerite's fragile palms and in his shouts to the midwife, the clerics, the priests, the peasants, the tenders of his vineyards and his hunting fields, the collectors of the tax. Your birth legitimised Brittany and everyone in whose veins ran Celtic blood shared in your birth, in your existence. Your life revived a nation. Thus you were revered from infancy until your last breath.

You knew this. You must have known. The serious beatification of your pale figure could have had no other cause. Though you desired, lusted and procreated as did any other – with the same fancies for enjoyment, wealth, and power – your love of poetry, beauty, song and your piety, my lady – the deep profound, overpowering religiosity of the child who strode through her father's duchy in wooden shoes to know the peasants' poverty – this child was our Breton duchess.

(Long pause)

Your legacy was so burdensome. I, the Epicurean scoundrel, could enjoy my weakness. But you, Anne, you were bewildered by yours and pained. But our infidelities are the least important part of this story. Perhaps when I am in prayer, repenting for my drunken bouts and thankful for the strength to satisfy my new wife's desires, I will reproach myself for my adulteries. But I will not allow them now to eclipse the euphoria of my memories.

(Louis XII moves slowly to the right forestage as the stage darkens, leaving him in semi-obscurity)

END OF SCENE II

SCENE III

LOUIS XII

I was a young prince favoured with wild strength, beauty and skill in riding, swordsmanship and battle, under the reign of King Louis XI, the Spider King, as he was appropriately named by our chronicler Philippe de Commynes. King Louis feared the possibility of my accession to the crown. His eldest daughter, beautiful yet arrogant, had beckoned my presence and attention; and mounted, with sword in hand, I had proved fiercer and more powerful in battle than Charles, the King's heir and youngest child, my cousin. Inevitably, therefore, King Louis's strategy was to humiliate and destroy my family, the House d'Orléans. The Spider King had become not only the enemy of Breton sovereignty, but my own antagonist.

(Lights come up slowly on the left, leaving Louis XII still in semi-obscurity on the right. As the scene of left stage lights up, the audience sees before them Louis XII's mother, head bowed, in curtseying position. The King – Louis XI – Spider King – who faces

the audience, appears as a stocky but ageing man with calculating, unbecoming features.)

DUCHESSE D'ORLÉANS

(The Duchess raises her head slowly, revealing to the audience that she is the same actress as the one playing Geneviève, costumed differently.)

Good morrow to Your Majesty! *(Gracious yet dignified)*

LOUIS XI

(Going to her and taking her hand)

Rise, my lady.

(Looks at her sombre attire)

More than a decade has passed since Charles d'Orléans ended his life. And you still wear mourning clothes. Where is the gaiety of the Burgundian court from which you are descended, Marie de Clèves?

DUCHESSE D'ORLÉANS

(ironic but respectful) Under your sword, my king. A people rarely remains spirited after conquest.

LOUIS XI

(Ironically, with nonchalance.) That, my dear, was a political necessity. The growing power of the brilliant Burgundian civilisation threatened France. *(Simply and fatalistically)* It had to be crushed. *(Changing the subject with simulated gaiety)* But that was another affair, unrelated to my cousin d'Orléans.

(Reflecting) Ah, Charles d'Orléans. Good men are too easily diminished. Your husband's fall from my favour would not have broken a stronger man. Ah, but he was a poet, Charles d'Orléans, your husband.

DUCHESSE D'ORLÉANS

In Your Majesty's court perhaps he sought a humble presence, but in his own he was master, dominant and respected. Louis, though more impetuous, adored him.

LOUIS XI

Your son, Louis, yes, my namesake and, as some say, my successor. The lad is growing. Was that not he who rode with my son Charles in the hunt at Troyes last summer? I hear talk of his prowess from my children. He is present at every one of the royal tournaments, bearing the Orléans banner, jolting most of my knights from their saddles. Most impressive. *(Feigning pleasure but with obvious resentment and suspicion)*

DUCHESSE D'ORLÉANS

He would be deeply flattered to know of your opinions, Your Majesty. He is already a strong competitor who offers no empty challenges. Louis fights to win.

LOUIS XI

So do I, madam. It is especially your son who has attracted my attention and thus my favour. And for this reason, I have asked you back again. Although the memory of my cousin's gay lyrics and poetry would have been enough to push me nostalgically to wish for the return of the d'Orléans family to my court *(pausing)*, I believe young Louis is ready to be married, as was my own boy some time ago. *(decisively)* I should like him to wed my daughter.

DUCHESSE D'ORLÉANS

(delighted and excited) Your Majesty honours our family. The Lady Anne has great charm and beauty and, as I understand, there is mutual respect and inclination.

LOUIS XI

It is not Anne de France he will marry, madam.

DUCHESSE D'ORLÉANS

(puzzled and surprised) My lord . . .?

LOUIS XI

I have two daughters. Anne will wed the Duke of Bourbon. Jeanne will marry Louis.

DUCHESSE D'ORLÉANS

(Stunned) Jeanne!. . . Your Majesty. . . I beg not to offend, but the jest, sir, is *(asserting dignified seriousness)* not kind. Jeanne is a saintly child, but greatly deformed. . . to the point that marriage is unthinkable and, perhaps, even cruel.

LOUIS XI

It is as I wish. *(matter of factly)* I have favoured Louis with Jeanne's hand. *(Repeating slowly and indulgently, as if to a child)* Louis will marry Jeanne.

DUCHESSE D'ORLÉANS

I beg you, sir, Louis would not choose to oppose your will. But the marriage you intend him for will extinguish the continuation of our own succession.

(Pause. Sudden revelation that this is the Spider King's intention, a look exchanged of mutual comprehension.)

It would be the end of or at least the critical weakening of the d'Orléans nobility, a branch of the royal family. *(insisting)* For generations, sir, we have helped to oppose your enemies: the rebellious lords of Burgundy, Brittany, Gascony and Aquitaine have failed to intimidate your royal authority – in great part, my lord, because of my husband's family.

LOUIS XI

Madam, until your husband died, he defied me. His final disobedience was to defend the cause of a traitor, a distant relative, it seems: the Duke d'Alençon.

DUCHESSE D'ORLÉANS

He defied the judgement of punishment by death, my lord. He questioned neither the principle of your authority nor did he deny the crime itself. He asked only for mercy and wisdom, as I ask of you now, sir, for my son.

LOUIS XI

And I reply to you now, madam, as I did to your husband. I care less than naught for such things.

DUCHESSE D'ORLÉANS

My husband spent twenty-five years in an English prison for having served yourself, my lord, and your father – for having served France.

(Changing tone as she regains composure, gentle but dignified and assertive) As you must know, sir, Jeanne, though virtuous and noble, could not bear healthy children. Though her capacities be great for spiritual and emotional love... she is not made for physical

consummation and pleasure. I beg Your Majesty – my son is a young man, of normal inclinations and desires. Do not punish him for the strength and promise he bears. He would not contest the succession of Prince Charles, your heir. He would serve you both with strength and humility.

LOUIS XI

Strength he has, madam. But humility is not in the blood of the d'Orléans family. *(determinedly)* Louis and Jeanne shall marry. The vows will be announced concurrently with those of Anne and the Duke of Bourbon.

(Louis XI rises and as he does, the Duchesse d'Orléans falls to her knees, attempting to plead again) Madam, do not debase us further with discussion of our children's sexual inadequacies. I run a government.

(Guard enters right at this moment)

GUARD

Sire, the carriage of Count Antoine de Chavannes, with the Princess Jeanne, has just passed through the gates.

LOUIS XI

Yes, I see them. All right, let them come up through the gardens. *(pausing)* Lady d'Orléans and I have completed our business. *(To the Duchesse d'Orléans)* That is all, madam. Later, you may embrace the princess who is to become Louis's bride.

(The lights slowly come up on left of the stage. A robust tall nobleman and counsellor to Louis XI, Count Antoine de Chavannes of Danmartin enters from stairs leading from the audience area, left downstage. He accompanies a woman, dressed in dark colours. The feminine figure is hunchbacked, with one hipbone protruding. The audience sees only briefly the deformed but hopeful face of the young woman as she turns to accompany de Chavannes across the garden.

The King watches as they approach through the gardens and mount the stairs)

LOUIS XI

My lord in heaven. She is hideous.

(As the two figures cross the garden, the lords and ladies whisper and point. De Chavannes stops Lady Jeanne midway and kindly places his cloak over her shoulders and lifts the cape over her so as to shield her face and body from ridicule and exposure to mockery)

LOUIS XI

God gave me two handsome children. Then he delivered this poor creature, twisted and deformed, born from nature's pain and rage. *(pause)* Unknowingly, she will serve me by her impotence and disfigurement. Louis will have no heir, none with the strength to contest my son's legacy and right to the crown. *(relaxing from the intensity of his glee and fear)* Now that this threat is crushed, I may attend to others who impede the tasks of consolidation. Brittany will soon belong to France.

(The lights slowly fade as Princess Jeanne and her escort reach the top of stairs, bow and kneel, facing the King. Their backs are at an angle to the audience, as King Louis XI turns his head towards the two figures at his left and calmly states)

LOUIS XI

Welcome, my daughter. *(arms outstretched towards her, feigning paternal affection)*

(Stage lights fade and leave entire scene in darkness. Immediately a light dimly illumines Louis XII sitting in the same chair and position as at the end of Scene II)

LOUIS XII

Unknowingly, the Spider King delayed the defeat of the rebellious Dukes of Brittany and Burgundy and their vast territories by making me his enemy. *(pause)*

I could not love Jeanne. The poor soul's company was unbearable, less so for her deformity than for the humiliation intended and imposed by our union. Nor could I regret not having Jeanne's sister, Anne de France, who, upon my rejection of her attentions, shared her father's pleasure in power and humiliation. *(longer pause)* I became the ally of François II, Duke of Brittany. Your father, Anne, had bade me visit his Breton court in Nantes. And there my angry debauchery and hopelessness were calmed by song, verse and friendship. I had found a refuge.

END OF SCENE III

SCENE IV

(Nantes, Brittany, before the château; the Duke Louis d'Orléans's cortège arrives and stops to the right of the moat and drawbridge, facing the audience. To the left are small thatch-roofed cottages, in front of and inside which peasant and artisans are busily labouring. Inside can be seen, heard and smelled a baker's shop and family. As the cortège approaches, the baker's son, a small boy, peeps out and races near, running after it excitedly. From inside another cottage can be heard and seen the clanking ironworks of a forger. In the open passageway between the forger's workshop and the baker's shop a woman operates a loom and an older man, with pipe and cap, carves a pair of wooden shoes. Towards the centre of the stage, to the side of the other cottages, vendors have been selling fruits, cheese, vegetables, poultry and rabbits. It is a market presently frequented by peasant farmers, merchants, servants, beggars and magistrates. Most are wearing recognisable Breton attire representing their respective classes. Others are wearing Parisian, Burgundian or English costumes. As the young baker's son chases and stares at the Duke's

carriage and cortège of noblemen and soldiers, another small boy sitting by his mother, the fruit vendor, plays the traditional Breton flute, dressed in the peasant blue cap and jacket typical of the period. Until the royal carriage is noticed by most, a young woman from a balcony in the blacksmith's cottage recites in Breton, while accompanied by both her own Breton dulcimer and the boy with the long Breton flute)

LADY

(reciting)

'Bai en Hennbont' zo un iliz

E' zo hanuiet er Baradoz

Er Baradoez e ma hanueit

O, nag he han' d'eus gouniet.

Un intanvez e oe Ker.' (4)

(The Duke dismounts, his horse held by his squire. The audience notes that it is a much younger Louis who appears before them, but the

same Duke d'Orléans of previous scenes. The Duke d'Orléans is dressed with simple elegance in the French aristocratic costume of the period. As he dismounts, he is recognised. Immediately, the commercial activity of the market and artisans slows down, in some cases is suspended; an expression not of reverence but rather curiosity and uncertain intimidation. Silence falls on all but the subdued voice of the woman with the dulcimer singing in Celtic. A merchant and servant woman bow, murmuring, "My Lord. . .")

DUKE D'ORLÉANS

Do you comprehend the Celtic tongue, William?

ACCOMPANYING NOBLEMAN

Nay, sire.

DUKE D'ORLÉANS

(Addressing the merchant nearby) You sir, I bid you good day!

MERCHANT

To you, my lord. *(bows)*

DUKE D'ORLÉANS

You speak French, you are an exception to the many Bretons I have encountered along the way from Blois to Nantes.

MERCHANT

I am a trader, my lord; among those Bretons whose living depends on commercial compatibility with the marketers of Champagne, Tours and Paris. *(Gesturing to the young woman reciting)* This is an old Celtic legend.

(As the merchant slowly tells the tale, the woman's voice continues, softly subdued in the background.)

[1]In the Breton village of Hennebout

There is a church named Paradise

---

[1] At this point, the woman begins her tale again, repeating the verses previously recited.

The Bretons, my lord, are fierce believers with strong traditions in religion and magic. So 'tis not surprising that Paradise could truly be incarnate on earth in their legends. Well, in this village, as I said, there is a church named Paradise as well deserves its name.

LADY

(reciting)

'Un intanvez e oe e ker

Hag e bede er chapel-se

Hi e bede(s) hag e ouile

'r verhicz vari(n') hi chileue.' (4)

MERCHANT

'A widow used to live in the town;

She used to pray in this chapel.

She prayed and prayed and wept

Until the Virgin Mary heard her.'

LADY

(reciting)

'Na me fried am eus kollet

N'am eus Ket boued de rein dehe

Lan eo ma zi e vugale

N'am eus Ket den'bet war er bed

Ret 'o d'ein laho 'nkai kohan

'benn soulajo er iaouan kan.'(4)

MERCHANT

'The widow declares as she prays and laments:

"I have lost my husband.

I have no one else on earth.

"My home is full of children.

I have naught withal to feed them.

I will have to slay the eldest

So the youngest may survive."'

LADY

(reciting)

'Intanvezig peur, n'en lahet ket

kerhet d'er ger, hui gauei boued

Hui 'gauei ar ho taul bara poezet

En ho parkeut segal hanvet (hanvecq)

En ho parkeut segal hanvet

Kai er re'rell 'divleua ket.' (4)

MERCHANT

The Virgin Mary responds to the widow's prayers and lamentations:

'"Poor widow, do not kill your child.

Run home – you will find victuals to eat.

You will find cooked bread on your table,

In your fields, summer rye.

In your fields, summer rye

And that of others has not lost its blossom."'

A song of hope, my lord; and belief.

DUKE D'ORLÉANS

Aye, a good verse. But so solemn. One is not pressed for solemnity before the last moment of life and, even then, sir, it is of little use. I myself, sir, seek knowledge from pleasure.

(Louis smiles and bows to the lady who had recited the verse. The lady inclines her head in response from her window. Her husband suddenly appears beside her, indignantly pushes her away from the window and closes the shutters. The Duke slowly mounts his horse as

his party follows him. He murmurs to Hailsham as he turns to lead his party across the moat towards the château, glaring back at the closed window.)

DUKE D'ORLÉANS

Mark the house, William. I may request a more private audience.

(In the distance can suddenly be heard trumpets. The lights fade and the stage remains in darkness for two to three minutes for scenery change. When the lights come up, Louis is crossing the drawbridge on horseback; the same child trails after him. Many of the townspeople have evidently followed him to the edge of the moat, the other side of the drawbridge from where the same cottages and workshops can be seen, having been moved to background. As Louis and his party cross over, the lights on the backstage where are the town and its buildings do not fade but are obscured and the lights come up on the rest of the forestage. The Chancellor Chauvin stands with two other noblemen at right forestage. The Duke of Brittany is with his finance minister further upstage, almost in the centre, on a diagonal line between

centre stage and the spot where Chauvin and his followers are. Marguerite, Anne and Françoise de Dinan are left forestage, facing François and Landais. Louis d'Orléans and his cortège of noblemen and soldiers pass by the two rows of trumpeters and banners representing the Duke of Brittany's Montfort dynasty. Louis's men carry the d'Orléans banner towards the left back of the stage at the edge of the moat. Upon passing through the formal welcome, Louis dismounts as a squire holds his horse. Courtiers bow as Louis and François approach each other.

DUKE FRANÇOIS II

As an ageing rebel to a stronger and younger ally, I welcome you, sir. You honour my realm.

DUKE D'ORLÉANS

You do me the honour, my friend. Before and after the Spider King's passing, you led the defence against French aggression. The

Montforts have well preserved the autonomy of Brittany. God grant you success against the manoeuvrings of the Beaujeu regency.

TREASURER LANDAIS

My lord, if I may. . .? *(hoping to be introduced)*

DUKE FRANÇOIS OF BRITTANY

Ah, yes, permit me to present to you, sir, my finance minister Pierre Landais. *(Landais bows, d'Orléans nods and thus acknowledges him.)* And my chancellor Guillaume Chauvin, whom you met, I understand, upon his final visit to the Spider's King's inquisition: I speak, as you know, of King Louis's displeasure at the news relayed by his spies in my court of an alliance between the English King Edward and myself. Ironically, it was Landais and myself, not Chauvin, of course, who had arranged the treaty. Unfortunately, it threw suspicion upon the credibility of our Chancellor Chauvin, who bore the blows of King Louis's anger in the course of diplomatic visits.

DUKE D'ORLÉANS

Yes, indeed, I remember. *(addressing Chauvin)* How goes it, sir?

CHAUVIN

Well, my lord. *(disarmed; Louis's attention and courtesy disrupts Chauvin's protective barriers of distance. Landais, who had hoped to dominate d'Orléans's attention, is displeased)*

DUKE D'ORLÉANS

I am most pleased to see you again, Chauvin. You held up well against the Spider King's battering. I do not share your Anglophobia but I do your love for France. Should I face imprisonment, your example will give me strength. *(Chauvin is by now completely disarmed and Landais very irritated.)*

FRANÇOIS, DUKE OF BRITTANY

Yes, Chauvin is my right-hand. But at times a bit inflexible. *(Taking d'Orléans aside)* In frankness, Landais has been of greater service of late in arranging diplomatic concessions with the English throne.

DUKE D'ORLÉANS

Chauvin is not a man to lose, sir. I would trade Landais's glib and talent for diplomatic compromise ten times over for an obstinate, honest man like your chancellor, But, pray, I see three fair ladies attending us, sir.

FRANÇOIS, DUKE OF BRITTANY

My lady Duchess Marguerite, my consort. *(Louis bows low with deep respect and kisses her hand)* Lady Françoise Dinan, Marquise de Laval, governess to our daughters. *(respectful bow from Louis)* And my joy and hope for the morrow, my heir and eldest daughter, Anne – Brett as we call her – future Duchess of Brittany.

(Louis bows low with the same reverence and respect he had shown to the Duchess Marguerite. He kisses her hand and observes her carefully. Anne is a young girl of nine, neat and solemn but deliberate and confident in manner.)

DUKE D'ORLÉANS

(Observing her seriousness) May I ask, my lady, how old you be?

ANNE

You may, sir. I am nine. I was born shortly after the Treaty of Senlis which safeguards Brittany from further French invasion.

DUKE D'ORLÉANS

You are well informed, my lady. Your future responsibilities have evidently aroused a masculine interest in politics. Ah, forgive me. We Franks have no women who inherit crowns or kingdoms. The Breton women are a stronger lot.

FRANÇOIS, DUKE OF BRITTANY

Come, sir, we have prepared your chambers and a plentiful meal for you and your party. After you have rested, you must join our gathering in the court. *(calls to the young boy at the passageway)* Squire!

(To Louis) Till evening, then, my family and my court bid you good appetite and repose.

DUKE D'ORLÉANS

Till evening, sir.

(François exits with his party. Louis d'Orléans stops to gaze at the river and sunset.) Come, William. A generous, beautiful sun still floats on the Loire waters, drifting and tilting what remains of sunlight. Let me bathe and feast. Then I would return to respond to the lyrical plentiful entreaties of our Celtic lass.

(Exeunt and lights go off)

END OF SCENE IV

SCENE V

Gaiety, conversation, victuals and wine are provided in the court of François, Duke of Brittany. Forestage left are Geneviève, whom the audience recognises in the costume of a courtier, and Sir William Hailsham, friend and companion of the Duke d'Orléans.

LORD WILLIAM HAILSHAM

Has the Duke returned from his nocturnal conquest? The court has been waiting nearly an hour for him to appear.

OCTAVE

He arrived back some time ago, sir. I helped to dress him for the evening. He seems in good spirits. The lady is a beauty. I had remained outside as my lord bade me, but her husband was at the market. The old fellow was bartering away his young wife's newly-spun wool.

LORD WILLIAM HAILSHAM

Keep an eye on your lordship, Octave. His new-found friends may not understand the Duke's rakish habits.

OCTAVE

Oho, I sense they do. With great respect, sir, the Duke of Brittany has his wife and his mistress in the same palace. His heirs mingle and play with his bastards before us now.

(Octave nods to the *group of children involved in serious play and lessons under the watchful eye of Anne's governess, Françoise de Dinan.)* The lady Dinan is the governess of Anne of Brittany. *(looking around, then whispering in confidence)* Lady Dinan and her brother, the Marquis de Gui, report regularly by messenger to the royal regent, Anne de Beaujeu. Dame Dinan and the Marquis plan that the Lady Anne of Brittany will marry the Marquis, to control Brittany, with the strength of French alliance.

LORD WILLIAM HAILSHAM

They are spies for France? *(pausing, moving closer in secrecy)* How do you know this, Octave?

OCTAVE

I have sources. The stableboy unknowingly brought a note to me, sir. He had found it as he unsaddled and groomed the horses this evening. The seal bore the arms of the Beaujeux. It had been broken but not by the boy who is, of course, illiterate. He quite naturally believed it was a message to Louis from the royal family. It was not. The Duke d'Orléans and his party were evidently not the only travellers of the day. I beg you, sir, as I did my Lord d'Orléans, to forgive my indiscretion.

LORD WILLIAM HAILSHAM

Show me the letter.

(Octave discreetly hands it to him. William reads it. After a minute or two he says:)

This is, as you say, Octave, proof of their intentions. It speaks even further of the Lady Antoinette Meignelais, her employment by the Spider King, Louis XI, as mistress to the deceased King Charles VII and now to Duke François II of Brittany. The Duke's lady was the Spider King's spy against his own father as well as against his rebel dukes.

King Charles had perhaps been right to fear for so long being poisoned by his son's agents. The Spider King wove a careful, strangling web of passion and trust.

OCTAVE

Yet, my lord, Lady Meignelais must truly love the Duke. She gave him children and seventeen years of her life, and openly lends him arms and gold. She is perhaps a courtesan whose former need of opportunism has been satisfied. Yes, Lady Meignelais must be content to lie in her Breton lover's bedchamber; and it must be, sir, that she is secure in knowing that, as long as Brittany does not fall, she will live until the end in luxury and affection.

LORD WILLIAM HAILSHAM

I will speak of this to Louis.

OCTAVE

Begging your pardon, sir, but I have shown him the letter. He is apprised of the intrigue now but has decided, sir, that it would be wiser to be informed and prudent rather than risk the loss of Brittany's friendship by denunciation of those whom Duke François most greatly trusts and loves.

LORD WILLIAM HAILSHAM

Yes *(reflecting)*, the letter, then, would not be proof enough. It could be considered a fabrication of those who wish to destroy all hope for reconciliation with France. I myself might question its validity. It could have been deliberately abandoned near our party by Chauvin's enemies. . . by Landais himself.

OCTAVE

Possibilities, my lord, which leave the Duke d'Orléans with no real basis for accusation, no concrete proof of treachery. Only probable facts with which he will prudently protect and further his own action.

(The Duke d'Orléans enters at this moment by the entrance close to Octave and Lord William Hailsham. As the Duke d'Orléans enters, the Lady Dinan looks up curiously from her absorption in Anne's embroidery. Octave bows and leaves as Lord William Hailsham joins the Duke d'Orléans. Hailsham hands the letter discussed with the Beaujeu seal to d'Orléans. The Duke receives it with a knowing smile. His eyes meet those of Dame Dinan who evidently recognises the letter. He looks at her steadily, and then moves towards the party of children surveyed by Dinan, near the fireplace.)

DUKE D'ORLÉANS

Madam, I bid you good evening.

DINAN

Good evening, my lord.

DUKE D'ORLÉANS

My servants found a letter they mistakenly believed to belong to me. Not bothering to check, I thoughtlessly opened and read it. The letter, madam, most certainly is not mine and must belong to you.

(Dinan and d'Orléans exchange meaningful looks. Dinan conveys fear as she is aware of the letter's compromising contents. D'Orléans conveys amused yet serious firmness. D'Orléans looks and listens to the children for a moment.)

Your influence on the children is most phenomenal. Anne, particularly *(gazing at Anne)*, has assurance and cultivation. She has the bearing of a duchess already.

DINAN

(Slowly recovering her composure and dignity) Indeed, sir, as is proper: that is what she be.

DUKE D'ORLÉANS

And in so being, the young woman's decisions and actions will always reflect freedom and independence of spirit, without intimidation. As long as she be so free, I will not oppose nor interfere with your guardianship. *(patting his pocket where he has placed the letter)* I am sure my lady understands.

DINAN

(Reddening) Yes, my lord, most assuredly so.

(As the Duke moves away, she shows dignified, controlled relief. D'Orléans approaches Anne, who had been reading Latin softly to Isabeau and her half-sister, Gabrielle, while the young boys play at marbles. D'Orléans listens to the recitation and her translation.)

ANNE

(Reads aloud in Latin the following passage with exceptional diction)

Janitor indigum dura

Religate catena,

Difficilem moto cardine ponde forem.

Quod precor exiguum est: aditu fac janua paruo

Oblicum capiat semiadaperta latus

Longus amor tales corpus tenuavit in usus. (5)

DINAN

(Interrupting and correcting)

Recite with more calmness and less passion, Anne. You are a scholar, not a comedienne.

ANNE

(Repeats the last line spoken before Dinan's interruption and suppressing much excitement as she speaks. However, d'Orléans is most drawn to her recitation and the subdued intensity with which Anne speaks. The meaning of the lines which Anne recites become significant and suggest the growing feeling between Anne of Brittany and d'Orléans.)

Longus amor tales corpus tenuavit in usus.

Aptaque subducto pondere membra dedit (5)

(Translates the above lines)

Caretaker who secures so vilely with a heavy chain. Have a difficult door roll upon its hinges. That which I request is very little:

arrange a small opening, so that the half-open door allows me to pass sideways. A long love so slimmed my body and thinned my limbs that I will be able to slip in thusly.

(Anne recites more of the same passage)
Ille per excubias custodum leniter ire
Monstrat; inoffensos dirigit ille pedes

At quondam noctem simulacraque vana timebam:
Mirabar, tenebris quisquis iturus erat. (5)

(Anne translates the above)
It is love who teaches one to tread calmly among one's guardians, it is he who directs one's steps and guards one from obstacles. In former times I feared the night and its empty phantoms, I admired all those who ventured into the darkness.

(Anne continues the passage.)
Risit, ut audirem, tenera cum matre cupido,

Et leviter: "Fies tu quoque fortis" ait.

(Anne translates)

He laughed loud enough for me to hear him,

Cupid did, accompanied by his loving mother.

Gently, he said to me, "You also will become bold."

(Anne continues the passage)

Nec mora, venit amor: non umbras nocte volantes,

Non timeo strictas in mea fata manus.

Te nimium lentum timeo; tibi blandior uni:

Tu, me quo possis perdere, fulmen habes.

Aspice, et, ut videas, inmitia claustra relaxa,

Uda sit ut lacrimis janua facta meis. (5)

(Anne translates)

Love came without delay: I no longer fear the shadows which come with stealth in the night nor arms borne for my ruin. That which I fear is to find you without feeling; it is you alone whom I cajole; it is you who bear the lightning with which you may crush me. Look, and in order to see it, open somewhat this cruel gate. How the door is completely moist with my tears!

(By the time Anne completes this passage, Louis d'Orléans is very moved. His emotion manifests itself in a subtle manner, with delicacy. Motionless as Anne finishes the passage, Louis d'Orléans makes a half turn away, meditatively)

DINAN

Very good, Anne. Soon, you will know more than our scribes.

ANNE

Thank you, Lady Dinan.

(speaking to Isabeau and Gabrielle) Did you note the eloquence of the work?

ISABEAU

But there was no joy in his love.

GABRIELLE

He who wrote the verse must have felt happiness in this new-found passion.

ANNE

Hear, sisters, another verse less hopeful but most profound.

(Translates from another work)

With time, the bull accustoms himself to the plough which labours the fields and puts forth his neck to the curved yoke which presses down upon him; with time, the fiery horse obeys the reins which hold him back and accepts the rough harness in his docile mouth; with time the anger of warlike lions is appeased and former wildness disappears; the Indian elephant obeys his master's orders, vanquished by time in slavery. Time swells the extended clusters of grapes and the grains retain little of their juice; time changes seed into withering clusters and causes fruit to lose its sharpness. . . Time can thus weaken all except my torment. Since I have been deprived of my country, twice the corn clusters were shaken into the air, twice the grape has burst, kicked by bare feet. However, such a long delay has not rendered me resigned and my mind experiences these evils as if they were recent. Thus often old bulls flee the yoke and often the tamed horse refuses the harness. . . (6)

(Anne thus ends her passage, in the course of which d'Orléans fixes his attention and his gaze upon her with melancholy intensity. His attention suggests a certain identification with the passage. The young Duchess Anne explains the background of the recitation to her sisters.)

The teller of the tale is in exile. *(Hailsham immediately exchanges a glance with d'Orléans, to suggest a similar political condition.)* The poet, Ovid, who had opposed the tyranny of Livia, wife of Augustus, recounts his experience as a hunted rebel. *(Again Hailsham glances furtively, suggestively at d'Orléans. D'Orléans nearby continues to gaze at the Duchess, with the beginning of a smile.)* There is beauty in his lyrics. . .

D'ORLÉANS

An obstinate rebel. His torment, was, thank God, not diminished by time. It gave him the strength to refuse tyranny. *(Melancholy)* I would welcome the same force of mind in exile. A true poet, indeed, Ovid, who does not wallow *(accepts wine from a servant)* in pathos. He reflects quietly, with compassion but defiance.

ANNE

(Surprised upon seeing and recognising the Duke d'Orléans.)

Good evening to you, sir. *(rises and curtseys)* My sister and I recite and sing in the early evening before the meal. *(presenting the others)* Do you know my sisters Gabrielle and Isabeau? His lordship Duke Louis d'Orléans. And these are Antoine and Claude, our brothers. *(The children bow or curtsey while Louis d'Orléans gives a reverential bow)*

ANTOINE

Have you seen our father, sir?

D'ORLÉANS

Not since early afternoon, my young lord. He will join us soon, I am sure.

(The Duke d'Orléans chatters among the children. Meanwhile Anne watches and listens absently as her sister plays the lute and the old troubadour in the corner plays the mandolin softly.)

ANNE

Here be Jehan Meschinot. *(Presents the old troubadour in the corner, isolated from the others, holding a mandolin.)* He is the poet and maître d'hotel of my father's court. His lordship the Duke d'Orléans, Monsieur Jehan. *(presenting the two men)*

D'ORLÉANS

There are none in my land who do not know of you, sir.

MESCHINOT

(Smiling humbly as he strums softly) Milord.

D'ORLÉANS

You are the poet who denounces the foolishness of the powerful princes, a brave thesis. Well beyond its time.

(Reciting)

'You who in your hands hold all your people

Pillaged as much in winter as in summer. . .

It is by displeasure, hunger and cold

That the poor die often.

It is without displeasure

That the lords among them go to war.

My lords: you regard us as rebels. . .

You only change Justice to brutality. . .' (8)

(Smiling sadly)

Perhaps, as you say in your verses, Meschinot, we are bound to face a reckoning.

(The Duke of Brittany enters with Madame Antoinette Meignelais on his arm)

DUKE OF BRITTANY

Welcome, sir; I hope you have rested well. My children, I see, provide good entertainment.

DUKE D'ORLÉANS

I am well rested, sir, and most impressed with your family. Anne, especially, is a most serious, profound child. She will be a true Duchess one day, my lord.

DUKE OF BRITTANY

Yes *(slowly, with happy pride)*, Anne is my treasure. We are, perhaps, too severe with her on matters of instruction, more than with the others, but there are obvious reasons for which Anne must be masterful in knowledge, reasoning and language.

(Remembering to introduce Madame Antoinette) Forgive me – my Lady Antoinette Meignelais, the source of all beauty that reigns in my home. His lordship the Duke, Louis d'Orléans.

MADAME ANTOINETTE

It is an honour, my lord *(bowing reverently)*.

DUKE D'ORLÉANS

(Lifting her by the hand which he kisses) One, Madame, which I profoundly share.

MADAME ANTOINETTE

Your Grace has come at a time most needed. The Bretons are wanting in allies.

DUKE OF BRITTANY

Ah, let us sup. Then we will talk of the Feudal League I have formed with Burgundy, Auvergne and Artois. And our friendship: let it be known that here you are and will always be welcome, as long as Brittany survives.

END OF SCENE V

SCENE VI

(The Duke of Brittany and the Duke d'Orléans enter. The Duke of Brittany goes to the table of the parlour to pour a special wine for them both. They are in the more intimately lit and furnished section of

the court's salon seen in the previous scene. It is late evening following a festive dinner.)

DUKE OF BRITTANY

You find Bretons warm, d'Orléans? *(while a servant resumes the pouring and replenishing of wine)*

DUKE D'ORLÉANS

I find your court cultivated, elegant and gay. I find the Bretons hardworking and, though intensely insular, with the exception of a few merchants, generous and warm. Their songs and their poetry reflect their loyalty to their race and to you, François. I have never before heard verses praising the past and God with such intensity. Not since my father read to me legends of Palestine.

DUKE OF BRITTANY

(Wistfully, in sadness and sudden fatigue) There has been so much war in this land; thank heaven we live in times devoid of quarrels with

the Orient. At least for a time. As I understand it, young King Charles dreams of French conquests in Italy and the Byzantine. Lord protect us from the fanatical ambitions of our rulers. Ah, well, he is still a boy under the thumb of the Beaujeu regency. That is one aspect of their influence upon him for which I am grateful. But it is the only one. *(Pause of a few seconds, and then, in answer to d'Orléans's previous remarks, says:)* Yes, the Bretons are pious Celts. It is part of their identity which helps them determine to go on living and to die without despair.

DUKE D'ORLÉANS

To die with hope is perhaps no better than to live with despair. There is, my friend, no less deprivation in your land than in France.

DUKE OF BRITTANY

Yes, we have our share of beggars and starving children. But you have seen in the course of your amorous pursuits the fine silks from Belgium, the English woollens, Spanish leather and the lace from

Lyon that our merchants, among the most prosperous of Europe, sell in our markets. We have the promise of prosperity with our industry and art.

While civil war ravaged France for the first half of our century, Brittany prospered. France's young King Charles VI was mysteriously driven insane; your grandfather, Duke Louis d'Orléans, the sole defender of the Dauphin's right to succession, was assassinated, and the French Kingdom invaded and plunged into civil war. And then the English invasion of your country, of France; your king, for whom your grandfather died, was disinherited by his mother and doubted the legitimacy of his own rights to succession. And when some maiden visionary-knight, Jeanne d'Arc, set everything right, drove out the English and ended civil war, when she was captured and condemned as a heretic, you French did nothing to save your national hero! You let your saviour burn.

We Bretons, however, lived for the first half of this century under the reign of my uncle, Jean V de Montfort, Duke of Brittany. While you French were living in fear and anarchy, Brittany evolved and flourished in a time of political stability. We in Brittany, with our one million inhabitants, survived our proximity to your warring nation. Normands fleeing the English and Spanish; Portuguese, German and Dutch refugees flock to Brittany and make their fortune in this golden age of our land. Our cities expand, our peasants and farmland are protected from unreasonable taxation, our commerce enriched by a lack of competition, given the mutual destruction of our enemies, France and England.

DUKE D'ORLÉANS

True, Brittany stands apart from the violence of our age. You have tried to live within a self-contained oasis for the last one hundred years. But even Brittany could not estrange herself entirely from the nightmare of The Hundred Years' War. Your uncle preserved Breton neutrality which spared your people the atrocities of war, for a time. But your dukedom, sir, like Savoy, Gascony and Provence, was a most dependable source of mercenary soldiers. The mercenary troops of your Armorican Peninsula indulged in pillages, murder, fire and rape. Thus, in my childhood, the word 'Breton' came to mean 'thief'. Most people were frightened by the terrorism emanating from prosperous Brittany. Still, these paid Breton warriors roaming the Alps and the Rhône valley were the most effective in combat. Many, as we know, proved to be invaluable leaders and tacticians for France. But it is well, my lord, and I above all recognise the sovereignty and dignity of your race.

Yet if you seek moral absolution for Brittany and deny your role in history, be it one of abetting violence or stabilising security and hope, I must respectfully remind you, sir, that, in the final analysis, we are all mercenaries of power.

(Long pause)

DUKE OF BRITTANY

My young lord, you have not lived long enough to distinguish absolutely innocence from guilt. But you have the brash cynicism of a lonely moralist, and such men as yourself can be consoled only by the pursuit of a truthful cause, however stained and impure that truth may be. *(Bending, gently towards him)* I will lend you my soiled truths if you should need them. *(D'Orléans inclines the head in emotion)* Come, drink with me and let us speak no more of history.

(D'Orléans takes the goblet and approaches the fire with François, Duke of Brittany. The two men sit on a settee, their profiles to the active fireplace in the back wall. They are facing each other, profiles seen by the audience, profiles darkened in contrast to the illuminating, angry fire in the background)

DUKE D'ORLÉANS

What of this league you have formed, François? Let us speak frankly. We are bound by a common adversary and rage against the present rule in France.

(At this point, Geneviève returns carrying a pitcher of wine to replenish the supplies in the men's goblets and resumes the sweeping that she was doing at the beginning of the play. As she moves forward, the silhouettes of the two men talking in the background darken. The two men speak for a bit more)

DUKE OF BRITTANY

La Ligue féodale, the Feudal League, is weakened by Burgundy's defeat, but we are strong enough for battle. I have two hundred thousand men. Charles, Duke of Guienne, has nineteen thousand. Before our defeat in Normandy and the Treaty of Senlis, we had well over six hundred thousand.

DUKE D'ORLÉANS

The French attack on the Loire was costly. Over three thousand men died, defeated.

DUKE OF BRITTANY

(correcting) Murdered, executed. A few were spared – those with family names and military stature. *(pause)* In any case, the League survived...

(At this point, the audience hears no more of their discussion. But Geneviève continues)

GENEVIÈVE

...The League survived... when my Lady Anne was born, the Spider King stamped and fumed and pouted, because he had had his way with everyone else but *not* with the Dukedom of Brittany. So he struck back. He revived a clause that had been revoked by Brittany's Parliament, a clause from the Treaty of Guérande, well before Anne of Brittany. That was back in the twelfth century, three hundred years ago. It was the treaty ending the terrible, bloody war of succession between the Montforts and the descendants of Charles de Blois of Penthièvre, three centuries before our Lady Anne. Since that time, the Montforts ruled *but* the outlawed clause stipulated that, should the Montfort Duke of Brittany have no male descendant, the dukedom would return to the Penthièvre family. After Anne was born, the Spider King was afraid. The most powerful of monarchs, Louis XI, was fearful of a newborn child. He thus thought to cut short her power. He revived this revoked clause of the Guérlande treaty. Then he purchased rights of succession from the last ageing descendant of the Penthièvre branch, Nicole de Bretagne and her husband. What a sly old fool! It did no good, you know, 'cause, as I said, our Breton Parliament had outlawed the clause.

DUKE D'ORLÉANS

(Continuing, but louder, as if there had been no interruption of his discussion with François) . . . in addition, sir, I have heard there is rebellion in your province. In recent months, many of the Breton barons have turned against you.

(Geneviève shakes her head and says "Aye!")

DUKE OF BRITTANY

Some rebel for ambition; others simply detest Landais, my treasurer.

DUKE D'ORLÉANS

Might I suggest that Landais be too dangerous and costly a liability? What provokes this hatred of your treasurer is costing you the unified support of your people who distrust the political trickery and manoeuvrings of a draper's son.

DUKE OF BRITTANY

What provokes this hatred of Landais is petty jealousy. He is practical and although too extreme in his tactics, he is a man I trust, implicitly. *(Geneviève shakes her head disapprovingly as she cleans)* Brittany's sovereignty could not have survived without his political expertise.

(Geneviève slams down her broom, removes her apron and, while wiping off perspiration, pours drinks again for the men. Then she comically drinks from the pitcher herself.)

DUKE D'ORLÉANS

Brittany may have drawn less antagonism had Landais been given less power to compromise. *(pause)* In any case, my dear sir, I am your friend. I will not abandon you.

(At this point Geneviève settles down to play the dulcimer softly while the men converse. The melody performed softly, slowly, is the fifteenth century Italian lute melody 'Mi ut re ut'. (9)

DUKE OF BRITTANY

I am gratified. But, dear Louis, we both are aware that each moment of honourable friendship ultimately has its price. You seek to liberate young King Charles VIII from the tyrannical regency of his sister, Anne de Beaujeu.

DUKE D'ORLÉANS

There is no dishonour in protecting one's king.

DUKE OF BRITTANY

Nor is there shame if such loyalty should coincide with one's own self-interest. *(pause)* I have heard that Charles is not strong and, torn between a tyrannical sister and a wilful cousin, will not rule many years. At that time, my friend, you would be crowned as his successor.

DUKE D'ORLÉANS

(Speaking as if to himself.)

You may believe that, François. I do not deny that conscious or unconscious ambition motivates my unfathomed dreams. Yes, I would be King. Yes, my friendship can be bought. I am a practical fellow who lusts and drinks and burns with bitterness, but my mercenary nature does not drive me to push my weak young cousin to the point of death. I remain enough of a man to respect the life of my king.

(Geneviève, in the background at this point, plays the same melody at a more intense, quicker rhythm and two young lovers perform a dance in the background, with sporadic moments of gaiety and melancholy)

DUKE OF BRITTANY

(Gently, as music and dancers have created a softer, more human mood.)

We are both angry souls. Still, as I intimated in prior discussions, the price of my support is Brittany's sovereignty and an end to French aggression. As your friend, I give you refuge from France. Yet, as your ally, I too have a price.

DUKE D'ORLÉANS

Agreed. Now we both admit to being scoundrels.

(Dancers leave, one pursued by the other. Louis watches them longingly. At this moment Pierre Landais enters, accompanied by Dunois, Louis d'Orléans's bastard cousin. Landais slowly moves beside his master, the Duke of Brittany. Symbolically, Dunois moves towards Louis d'Orléans)

DUKE OF BRITTANY

(To Pierre Landais) Have the children been put to bed, Pierre?

LANDAIS

Yes, sir. The Lady Antoinette awaits you.

DUKE OF BRITTANY

Yes, I am very tired. *(gets up slowly, wearily. Turns finally to Louis d'Orléans, moving close)* The cause is not lost, my friend. On the morrow we will plan a more careful strategy. Upon parting for the evening, let me assure you, if you promise protection for Breton freedom – that we be safe from the ambitions of the French Valois king – I will promise you my continued support and that of the Ligue féodale.

DUKE D'ORLÉANS

You have my word, sir, that I will seek to protect Brittany.

DUKE OF BRITTANY

We will speak more on the morrow, sir.

(He turns to leave. Geneviève stops playing and gets up with relief and fatigue. She puts down her dulcimer. She quickly takes the goblets from the two men and bends to pick up the pitcher. Interrupted by Pierre Landais's voice.)

LANDAIS

Your pardon, my lords.

(Geneviève shrugs her shoulders with disappointment and, out of frustrated fatigue, takes another swig from the pitcher of wine.)

May I ask – have you discussed the matter of my Lady Anne's marriage? *(embarrassing silence)* Your daughter, sir, and the choice of husband.

(François is surprised and embarrassed and Louis puzzled by Landais's remarks.)

DUKE D'ORLÉANS

Of what relation. . .?

DUKE OF BRITTANY

(breaking off Louis's speech) Pierre, that is for another day. The matter of my daughter's marriage is too important to be discussed by two weary men.

(Louis now with amused suspicion observes laconically the two men.)

LANDAIS

(To Louis) Would it not make your professed friendship, sir, a certainty to receive the hand in marriage of Anne, Duchess of Brittany?

(François, further embarrassed, tries to interrupt and quiet Pierre, but Landais is too cunning) Would it not be a joy to have such a wife, a duchess, revered and quite attractive, whose inheritance of the duchy of Brittany would bring you greater power and, certainly, greater ease in political alliance? *(Turning to François)* And you recall, my lord, you eagerly agreed that we should propose this arrangement, to safeguard Brittany.

DUKE OF BRITTANY

(slowly and wearily) Yes, indeed, but I did not choose this moment. You have disobeyed my wishes.

LANDAIS

Do forgive my impulsive wish to protect my lord and my homeland, sir. Surely, if the Lady Anne should accompany his lordship in royal succession and become his queen, there would be great glory for Brittany.

DUKE D'ORLÉANS

(finally interceding) And for Brittany's ministers, I imagine...

(Landais turns like a shot and meets knowingly the eyes of the Duke d'Orléans, but maintains a humble, cunning demeanour. Geneviève again laughs and shakes her head in agreement, saying, "Aye, aye." She meets Pierre's glare with equal hostility.)

DUKE OF BRITTANY

(Caressing Pierre's hair and placing his hand on his shoulder as he speaks.) Come, Louis, we are all practical sinners.

(Fondles Pierre's chin and cheeks with his hand, at which point Louis and Geneviève look at each other with comprehension of these gestures.) My minister speaks out of turn. *(Pierre gestures protest)* But he does speak for me. What of it? Anne is by far the more promising prospect for a pleasing union assuring political alliance.

DUKE D'ORLÉANS

There are impediments. I am married.

DUKE OF BRITTANY

Yes, that is another cross you bear. Lady Jeanne is a kind soul but, from what you tell me, it was a union forced upon you by the Spider King, that there may be no children from such a joyless marriage.

LANDAIS

It is, as I understand, not consummated. *(Said with artful insolence)*

DUKE D'ORLÉANS

(Shocked by Landais's remark and offended) What gall your man has to speak to me of such a matter!

LANDAIS

Only practical honesty, my lord. It is a useful fact and a convincing one, should you choose to divorce.

DUKE D'ORLÉANS

Divorce Jeanne! The woman may be the instrument of a perverse man's power, but... my inability to love her – my carnal infidelities – have given that generous lady unwarranted pain... *(appears to think of another obstacle)* But you have forgotten... what of the alliances you have previously arranged with the Duchess Anne as your pawn? She is to be the bride of the young Edward V of England. And perhaps even to the Tudor pretender to the English throne, Henry of Lancaster. Ah, but Maximilian, the Austrian Emperor, has received your approval to marry Lady Anne as well. And Charles, my cousin, our King of France, has received from you messages implying your consent to a *royal* marriage for Lady Anne. And what of Dunois *(pointing to him)* and the other Breton noblemen?

DUKE OF BRITTANY

Yes, I have found political support far and wide. I am a pragmatic leader. Everyone has an eye on Brittany and I spare no means to exploit those who covet my land. Yet the only true contender, the only one to whom I have officially promised Anne's hand without equivocation, is Edward IV's son, the heir to the English throne.

DUKE D'ORLÉANS

And Henry of Lancaster?

(Landais squirms uncomfortably for, without François's knowledge, Landais is planning a marriage between Henry of Lancaster and Anne of Brittany)

DUKE OF BRITTANY

Only possibilities, no sworn agreement.

LANDAIS

Shall we say, that should you, sir, succeed your cousin before young Edward does his father, you, sir, will have a greater right to the Lady Anne's hand, if you should find a legal way to marry her.

DUKE D'ORLÉANS

(Pause) It will be years before I succeed my cousin. I will not push him to his death. *(pause)* But I will abide by the terms of our engagement, sir. For Charles, for Brittany and for revenge – I give you my word, François.

DUKE OF BRITTANY

As do I, Louis, promise to you alliance and friendship, unequivocally.

(Silence follows. François reaches for both Louis's hands. Pierre stealthily bows in retreat, and we hear his voice calling to Lady Meignelais)

LANDAIS

My lady, the tedious discussion has ended. The Duke will attend you presently.

(Exeunt the Dukes, unaware that Anne of Brittany has entered, quietly standing in her night-clothes by the hall, seen by the audience only moments before the men leave by right stage. Geneviève is putting on her apron and resuming her sweeping. The audience does not know that Geneviève is aware of Anne's presence. Geneviève, because of her stout form and quickened movements, breathes heavily)

ANNE

They have planned every detail. I an to be their instrument of immortality. *(Listing)* Louis's unhappiness will be avenged. Landais's ambitions will be nurtured and my father's Brittany will remain intact. And I – I will have so many husbands. *(matter of factly, without bitterness)* Louis is quite right. I *am* a pawn. *(pause)* Which one will I really marry, Geneviève?

GENEVIÈVE

Go to bed, girl. You'll be a duchess and far stronger and better than all of the three, I can tell you that. *(pause)* Marry, child? Why should you care which one is chosen as your husband?

ANNE

Whom will I marry ? Tell me, Gen – you who know what the end of the story will be. You who know the author of this play.

GENEVIÈVE

Ssh, you'll destroy all illusions. *(Embarrassed)* And no, I don't know everything that's to happen. But neither does the author. This may be a lovely version of your life story, my lady, but it is not an author's invention, it is history. No one's creative power will predict or change it. *(pause)* But why should the choice of husband be of such great importance to you? You will be a great duchess and perhaps a queen, with greater strength of mind than any husband of yours could bear.

ANNE

I am still a child, Geneviève, and, as such, subject to romantic visions but, beyond that, it is accurate to assume that the choice of a lifelong companion determines where I will go, what I will do and how I will do it. Will it be Edward, Prince of Wales?

GENEVIÈVE

Poor lad! There's a pawn for you.

(Anne looks alarmedly and distrustfully at Geneviève.)

ANNE

Will it be Maximilian of Austria?

GENEVIÈVE

Imagine – you an Empress! Who would take care of Brittany?

ANNE

Will be it be Lady Dinan's brother, the Marquis de Gui?

GENEVIÈVE

He is a bit old for you, love, don't you think? Of course, this will depend on your own inclinations. If it were me, I'd never share a bed with such a man. He snorts and belches.

ANNE

(Impatiently) Will it be Charles, King of France? Or Louis, Duke d'Orléans?

GENEVIÈVE

(Mischievously) Why, which do you fancy more, Lady? *(Anne reddens)* What was this you said of feeling as if you were a pawn. . .? *(She laughs boisterously, a little wickedly. She bends down*

to Anne and lifts her above her head)* Ah, come now, you'll marry well but you'll be strong. What more could you really wish to know?

ANNE

(Pursuing her advantage) And my father. . . he won't give in to Landais, will he? He won't be influenced by that man's twisted ambitions. . . Tell me. . . and my mother?

GENEVIÈVE

Anne, *(sadly)* you can't be told all before it happens. Come on, to bed with you! *(looking quickly at the audience)* These folks are waiting to stretch their legs before we go on with the story. You'll have all questions answered as you live your life yourself. It would mean nothing for me to tell you either truth or fabrication. Come on now, intermission is waiting!

ANNE

(Anne leaves, turns with uncertainty, then, with a sad, profound but confident smile on her lips, touches Geneviève's arms gently and says:)

Good night, Geneviève.

GENEVIÈVE

Good night, my lady. . .

(Anne exits. Geneviève slowly, somewhat moved by the melancholy of the young duchess, resumes her sweeping. Then, taking note of the audience again, she says)

Ah, yes. . . well, you probably would like to rest a bit, search out refreshment or feel some fresh air while exchanging viewpoints on the play. Don't mind me, I've got more to do. See you in a bit.

(Geneviève slowly turns her back to the audience and keeps the same rhythm as before, sweeping towards backstage. The lights dim slowly as she walks towards backstage.)

END OF ACT ONE

(As Act One ends, and curtains close over the stage, musicians below perform Vivaldi's 'Concerto for two violins, strings and basso continuo in B minor'. (10) *It is a performance of approximately seven minutes, allowing an additional ten minutes' intermission for musicians as well as the audience)*

ACT TWO

SCENE I

(A year and three months later, in the summer of 1485, Château de Nantes. Later in the scene, lights will simultaneously illumine rooms within the castle on a higher level – specifically the Duke's parlour, and the bedroom of Duchess Marguerite, his wife. Both rooms will be lit at special moments. As the curtains open, one sees faint lights in the courtyard. A guard stands at command beside torch lights within the wall surrounding the upper level. Another younger guard stands at attention nearby, outside the closed door of the tower prison. This latter guard is not in the service of the Duke as the mutual distrust between the two men reveals. He breathes quickly, as if out of apprehension or fear, as he watches steadily the Duke's guard, calmer, nearly lethargic – so accustomed is he to his nightly duty. After a minute, the wooden door of the tower prison creaks slowly open. The Prince d'Orange, obviously the master of the latter guard,

climbs down the steps of the tower and emerges with his comrade from the wooden prison door held open by one of his party. The creaking of the door and the steps of the descending men are very clearly heard by the audience who perceives the action on a very dimly-lit stage. As the nobleman emerges on to the stage, he does so in a daze. Stirred by the fresh summer air, he shakes himself and slowly we see him seize his sword which he thrusts into the sky and then into the ground; he then hunches over his weapon, face looking towards the ground and stares with emotion. One of his comrades, Maréchal de Rieux, places a hand on his shoulder and speaks to console and to articulate the outrage the Prince d'Orange's party has just witnessed)

MARÉCHAL DE RIEUX

Chauvin loved the Duke too much to have died in this way. Starved by Landais, the most honourable Breton is nothing more than a neglected corpse and a feast for rats.

PRINCE D'ORANGE

(Regaining his composure, with same sadness still, he turns to his guard) Inform the castle watchman that we, Lord Chauvin's closest of friends, will return with a priest to bury him mercifully. You four will remain behind to guard the body of our friend and to assure that no guards are aroused before our return.

(Shouting to the guard) Lower the drawbridge.

YOUNG GUARD

Yes, sir.

(The young nobleman's guard takes the lance from the palace guard who, amazed, submits entirely. He bids his unknowing comrades to lower the drawbridge. When the drawbridge is lowered down from the back of stage, revealed to the audience is a moat and countryside in the distance. The nobleman and his party leave, moving towards the back of stage over the drawbridge. The palace guard and the young, nervous guard of the nobleman eventually begin

to converse. The palace guard is an older type who sits wearily upon a bench against the palace wall)

PALACE GUARD

Lord Chauvin, then, is dead. Unbelievable. His lordship Landais was charged with Chauvin's care and nourishment.

YOUNG GUARD

He could not have seen food for weeks. He was shrunken in form, deliberately starved.

PALACE GUARD

The Duke could not have known. He would not have let this happen. But after the trial, Chauvin was put in Landais's charge. Landais had denounced him and, from what I hear, he had brought forth documents and witnesses to prove that Lord Chauvin had betrayed Brittany for better fortune with France. Lad, I do not like the Lord Treasurer Landais, but he soundly proved Guillaume Chauvin's treachery.

YOUNG GUARD

My master, the Prince d'Orange, does not believe Landais's accusations. He was in Normandy when Chauvin was condemned; he could do nothing but protest vainly. I knew his lordship Chauvin. He fed my family during the last rebellion although we were on opposing sides. And now we find him starved by those he served.

PALACE GUARD

I would have seen to him, had I known. He was a crusty old man but worthy and respected. *(pause. Then, sadly)* God help Brittany.

YOUNG GUARD

If this be the protection you offer those you judge worthy and considerable, indeed, sir, God help Brittany. Landais will pay on all accounts. If not tonight, some day. *(to the palace guard, gently)* Sleep, old man. They will return in an hour or so.

(Lights fall for a minute then turn on again. Voices are heard. The Prince d'Orange and his party have returned, stirring the guards from their slumber. The young guard stands and calls:)

YOUNG GUARD

Lower the drawbridge!

(The drawbridge is lowered. From the other side of the moat, the nobleman is seen on horseback with about twenty other Breton and Norman noblemen, accompanied by their squires. They descend from the horseback and move across the drawbridge, coming towards the audience. There is a young priest with them)

YOUNG GUARD

This way, mon père.

(Leading the cleric into the tower, the drawbridge remains down. The noblemen draw their swords and turn to climb the palace wall towards the Duke's quarters. The old guard tries to stop them but is pushed aside. The other two guards, unaware of the evening visitors, are disarmed by the nobleman's party and locked in a chamber where the rest of the Duke's guards are supposedly sleeping. Two of the Prince d'Orange's men stand guard outside this door, with lances drawn. Only muffled men's voices are heard within: the Duke's guard awakening and protesting. The older palace guard has been ignored, however, and stealthily runs across the drawbridge towards the nearby town to seek help for the Duke. No notice is taken of him by the noblemen, who consider him harmless. Slowly and brutally, the gate of the Duke's palace is broken down by the nobleman and his angry party. Lights come on in the upper level, first in the Duke's chambers, where we see him in consultation, and then in the Duchess Marguerite's parlour where Isabeau and Anne say their evening prayers in the presence of Duchess Marguerite and Lady Dinan, their governess. As the Duke and his family look towards the audience, to

comprehend the intrusion, their faces and gestures exhibit controlled fright and confusion. The noblemen burst into both rooms – the Duchess's parlour and the drawing room as well. We see that the rooms are lit by candelabra. Slowly the other rooms of the castle are lit up, as the noblemen enter them in their search. As they leave each room, the room fades again into darkness.)

PRINCE D'ORANGE

(Entering the Duke's parlour) Your pardon, my lord.

DUKE OF BRITTANY

How came you here? 'Tis an unlawful intrusion. Do you know the penalty for—?

PRINCE D'ORANGE

(Cutting him off) Chauvin is dead. We have seen his body – rat-bitten, unrecognisable. Now, we seek Landais. *(As he speaks,*

noblemen search the drawing room and the chambers of the duchess-to-be)

ANNE

(Watching indignantly, yet fascinated despite her fright) He is not under my bed, sir.

(The nobleman searching under the bed looks up, surprised, at her and reddens sheepishly. Not waiting for an angry response, Lady Marguerite seizes her daughter's hands and pulls her along as she seeks out her husband. The Duke, seeing his wife and children beside him, followed by the governess, speaks steadily to his valet, while moving to pour himself a glass of wine)

DUKE OF BRITTANY

Bring my lady's shawl, Jacques. The night has brought a chill and she shall not fall ill again.

(He says to Marguerite) **They seek Landais. Chauvin has been found dead in the tower.**

PRINCE D'ORANGE

(To Lady and Duke) Our apologies for the intrusion but as soon as Landais crawls out from his hiding place we will leave with him.

MARGUERITE

Chauvin! How! No, it isn't true. The unfortunate man, ruined by us all. My husband was forced by proof of betrayal to imprison, not to torture or murder.

PRINCE D'ORANGE

We seek Landais. Only him.

ANNE

(Turning to her father) Father, why did we not know of Monsieur Chauvin's condition? Where is Landais?

(Turning to soldiers, ironically) Did you look everywhere possible – in the offices, in the private chambers, in the cupboards, next to the mice? He sometimes carries on with Mathilde, the chambermaid; perhaps he's under her bed.

LADY MARGUERITE

Anne! No more!

(Isabeau laughs nervously and the noblemen are amused.)

ANNE

(Looking uncomprehendingly and angrily at her father) Monsieur Guillaume Chauvin was innocent, definitively ruined by Landais's fabricated evidence of treachery. Why could we not have listened at least to your ally, the Duke d'Orléans, when he pleaded in Chauvin's

favour? Why, father, all those many months ago did you allow Landais to decide Chauvin's treatment?

DUKE OF BRITTANY

(Angrily) That is enough, Anne. I granted Guillaume his life. Prison was the lesser punishment.

ANNE

There was no mercy for him in Landais's charge. Did you never see the hatred in his eyes for him? Chauvin, under Landais's care – it was less kind than death. *(pause)* We did not protect the man.

DUKE OF BRITTANY

Anne, you will quiet yourself. *(At the point of an ultimatum in dealing with his daughter. Then, adding:)* Landais is my friend and absolutely faithful servant.

(Turning to the noblemen) If Landais is guilty of perjury, torture and murder, as you say, sir, it is my government that will try him

fairly and determine if there are crimes for which he should pay. Until we have done so, I answer to no one. *(pause)* I bid you withdraw. If Landais is guilty, he will be punished. Withdraw, sir, before it is too late.

PRINCE D'ORANGE

Respectfully, your lordship, I fear that your friendship for this man is blind. We will distribute justice to the draper's son.

(Voices and shrill cries are heard below and the audience sees and hears the approach of a crowd of townspeople carrying sticks, swords and pitchforks, and moving across the drawbridge. The crowd shouts angrily that they will protect their Duke. They threaten, by their cries, to hang the noblemen)

DUKE OF BRITTANY

Our people have other plans. *(gloating yet pleasantly surprised by his people's protection)*

PRINCE D'ORANGE

(panicked by the crowd's threats) It is well. We will leave in peace, for a time. Tell them we will leave with our friend's remains, to bury him.

DUKE OF BRITTANY

(Hesitates, but then decides himself. He moves to the balcony and calms the people by his presence)

My Bretons, we are unharmed, safe and in peace. Our guests have lost a friend, a political prisoner, who passed away last evening. They came to punish my minister whom they cannot find. They have threatened us with neither violence nor submission; but they mourn their friend and wish to bury him. *(pause)* I beg you, let them leave to do so. *(sound of the crowd, undecided, distrustful)* We have all agreed to determine guilt another time. Let them *leave Brittany in peace*.

(At this last phrase, the Prince d'Orange looks up, realising François's clever way of imposing exile. He looks at Anne, who looks down, ashamed of her father's ploy)

PRINCE D'ORANGE

So, we have been exiled.

DUKE OF BRITTANY

Would you prefer to face the anger of this crowd without protection?

PRINCE D'ORANGE

So be it, sir. For a time.

(To Lady Marguerite) Madame, my humble apologies.

(To Anne) You, young princess, have the wisdom to recognise evil.

ANNE

Nay, my lord. I know not what evil is, nor where in the human body or soul it takes root, nor at what moment in life one may take its measure and say, 'In truth, I have measured this person, who causes pain, who destroys; and although he brings strength and affection to some *(looks at her father, compassionately, who turns his head away)* he must be evil.' *(pause)* Nay sir, I, like you, am repulsed by the ravages of one man's sins. But I know not how to recognise <u>evil</u>. I have not the wisdom. *(pause)* Do you, sir, know where it hides, so that we may bundle it up and expunge it from ourselves and have it destroyed?

PRINCE D'ORANGE

(Taken aback but answers) Yes, my lady: wickedness will be slain when Lord Landais swings from a rope.

ANNE

And why, sir, will he hang?

PRINCE D'ORANGE

For the cruel murder of Chauvin!

ANNE

And cruelty and murder *are* evil?

PRINCE D'ORANGE

Aye, *(as if talking to a naïve child, indulgently)* my lady.

ANNE

Then, sir, *(pause)* who will hang you?

PRINCE D'ORANGE

(Smiles, ironically, appreciating the young girl's wit. He bows and kisses her hand) My lady. I am your servant.

(Bows and leaves the Duke's chambers. Walks into the stairway and begins to descend, facing the audience and followed by the others) Fetch the priest and what remains of Chauvin.

(His followers do as he bids, moving carefully before the murmuring, tense crowd. They cross the drawbridge to the other side of the moat, where their squires meet them with their horses; they mount and ride off in the distance. Only the creaking of the tower prison door breaks the silence. Slowly the lights turn down on the motionless crowd and the characters until the stage is in darkness)

END OF SCENE I

SCENE II

(Anne and her father, months later. The Duke of Brittany reads aloud the following letter from King Edward IV of England)

DUKE OF BRITTANY

'I, Edward, King of England, request of thee, François, Duke of Brittany, that, as my friend and ally, you deliver unto me my hostile enemy, Henry of Lancaster, who presently enjoys refuge in your land.'

(One hears noises and voices from an open corridor which shows Henry of Lancaster drinking and charming courtesans)

'Only when Henry is safely contained by my forces might it be possible to resolve the Wars of the Roses and secure stability in my kingdom. Only when Henry and his rebels are suppressed will England have the strength and inclination to protect Brittany from French aggression. I bid thee remember as well the marriage agreed upon between my son, Edward, Prince of Wales, the future English monarch, and your eldest daughter, Anne. There is rumour deftly communicated to me that an insidious influence upon you is encouraging the possibility of marriage between Anne of Brittany and Henry of Lancaster and subsequent Breton assistance in the seizure of the English throne. I bid thee, François, to honour my government and our alliance. Deliver my enemy to me and I shall not abandon the Bretons.'

(François, Duke of Brittany, sits vacantly in silence. Anne, slightly older, an adolescent of thirteen, of graceful demeanour, approaches him, having overheard the letter's reading. François does not see her approach. She stops midway and curtseys, with head still bowed)

ANNE

Will Sir Henry be returning to England soon, father?

DUKE OF BRITTANY

(Jarred from his reflection) He will leave Brittany as soon as time and the sea winds allow.

ANNE

Then he will not be my husband and my engagement to the Prince of Wales is still valid. *(excitedly, she approaches her father)*

DUKE OF BRITTANY

(Smiling and caressing her hair) He is most cultivated and knowledgeable, Henry of Lancaster. It is Landais's ambition that Sir Henry leads a successful revolt against King Edward and rises to the English throne, with you at his side. And yet, *(gesturing towards the letter)* Edward reminds me of the word I gave him, that you would become the bride and queen of the legitimate heir to the throne, the Prince of Wales. *(pauses, looks at Anne, then says reassuringly)* No, Anne, Henry of Lancaster will not be your husband. *(He smiles at Anne's obvious relief.)* Would such a union be so undesirable, Anne? If Henry returns to England he *could* overthrow King Edward and reign as his successor. And you, my little Brett, will have lost your chance to be an English queen.

ANNE

You gave me lessons, father, long ago, on the honour and independence upheld by our family through two centuries of rule. How many songs and legends Madame Dinan and the old servant woman, Geneviève, used to drum into my head about the bloody War of Succession between ourselves, the Montforts, and the House of Blois. *(seeing her father's amusement)* Yes, I know, these were child's tales and legends, passionate and heroic. But your indoctrination taught me to defend our family's honour as the legitimate rulers of Brittany. *(pause)* Whether you know it or not, father, you have taught me to respect a certain truth. How, then, could you have me forget the legitimate rights to the throne of young Edward of York, Prince of Wales? Yes, Henry is very charming and amusing in the court although he knows no poetry, like Louis. He is a politician, father, whose only inclination to my person is motivated by the power I would bring him as duchess: the power to rule Brittany, to defeat France and to ascend the English throne. Landais would have it so, but it will not be. *(looking carefully at her father with compassion and perception)* Are you thinking, father, that Henry might die if you send him back to face King Edward?

DUKE OF BRITTANY

Edward would not let him live, I am afraid. Lancaster is the greatest threat to him.

ANNE

And yet to let him stay would nullify our political treaty and alliance with England, which we need desperately. To choose between obedience to an ally and death to a friend is a task I do not envy you, father.

(She heads towards the door which is very far from them both. Then she turns after a sudden stop and says with determined inspiration) We'll send him away, but not to England. We will have met our obligation to Edward by refusing to harbour our political adversary and yet we will have saved him from Edward's revenge.

DUKE OF BRITTANY

My little Brett, what of the truth you urged me to respect? Should I not teach my duchess how a ruler chooses between duty and life?

(laughs and says to Anne:) Yes... *(pausing)* that is what we shall do, most intelligent Anne.

ANNE

(Turns as she listens to her father's decision) That is the only way. But Henry *will* get to England with or without our help, to face his assassins. And if Henry should survive and overthrow King Edward, what will become of the young Prince of Wales, heir to the English throne?

DUKE OF BRITTANY

Would you have me kill Henry to prevent a political struggle that threatens your fiancé, Anne? A child ruler must sustain the violence of an ambitious aristocracy. *(Actor's interpretation of this last line indicates it is advice to Anne more than concern for the English heir)* Young Edward has more enemies than he does friends. *(pause, sadness)* But I fear that the boy may not live to be crowned, whether or not Henry of Lancaster returns to his homeland.

(Sounds of church bells and Gregorian chants heard faintly in the distance)

Let us kneel, Anne, it is time for your prayers.

END OF SCENE II

SCENE III

(An inn to the north of Blois; as curtains rise, audience sees the interior in darkness. The lights first come up upon a man's arm wielding a heavy knife and letting it fall. We hear only silence until the knife slams down upon a wooden surface, at which time the silence is interrupted by the noise of its fall and the laughter of people – clients in the inn. The moment it falls, the rest of the stage is lit up. We see that the scene is the interior of a lively inn. The man wielding the knife is obviously one of the cooks cutting up meat for supper. To the right of the stage, he continues to heave the instrument at intervals (behind a partly cut-off area) in preparation of the evening meal and,

as the stage lights up, the noises of other activity in the room overshadow but do not drown it out. There are open Norman-designed windows in the left back wall of the inn through which we can see countryside, horses and carriages. To the left and centre upstage and downstage we see wooden benches and tables, most of which are vacant except for five or six people – two women and three men supping and drinking from wide-brimmed goblets. They are of the bourgeois class. An older manservant working for the inn walks quickly to and fro, serving wine and food. To the centre, one sees the party of the Duke d'Orléans, attended by two courtiers. The character we know as Geneviève comes in from a passage proceeding from upstairs at back, upstage seen through an open door. As she passes on to the stage and is seen by the party, Louis nods mischievously to his courtiers who bow and discreetly move away and exit. Geneviève comes forward and bows slightly to Louis and his companion. Geneviève is evidently in this scene the proprietor of the inn. She is, as before, plump, buxom, but more attractively attired)

GENEVIÈVE

(curtseying) My lord Duke d'Orléans.

DUKE D'ORLÉANS

(Wearily) Good evening, madam. *(rising and kissing her hand)* I have run away again, I am afraid, from the reins of Charles's regents.

(As Louis speaks, we see he has already drunk quite a bit) The King's hunting quails this afternoon to escape his regent sister's stifling, gayless court. I left his party a few miles back. My Lady Jeanne is saying her prayers, forgiving me again most probably for a fruitless sexual arousal. The regents are, I imagine, sticking pins in a faded image of my likeness. I journey to the festival at Rennes this evening and hope to sup and rest here, should you choose to provide me with succour.

(Looking her up and down with nonchalant desire) Your husband is well, Madeleine?

GENEVIÈVE

Yes, indeed, but my lordship knows *(looking at him with understanding and amusement)* that my spouse absents himself at the end of every week to sell our wines. I alone welcome my lord and attend earnestly to his pleasure. Do you wish, sir, to dine here while we prepare your rooms?

DUKE D'ORLÉANS

There might be a more comfortable abode.

(Geneviève laughs and takes Louis's arm. As they proceed, back to the audience, arm in arm, they move towards the back passageway right back centre stage from where Geneviève had come down the stairs)

All I require at this moment is good meat, a few bottles of claret and a friendly lady with lungs and breasts to laugh, to smile, to satisfy.

GENEVIÈVE

Come now, sir, you know that I have no difficulty in satisfying the needs of my customers and, most particularly, my friends.

(calls to one of the cooks) Richard, bring our meals to my quarters.

(Lights fade. The stage is in darkness for no longer than three minutes. Then slowly the lights come up. The entire stage is in semi-darkness. It is evening. Only an open door at the back of right centre stage shows a bedroom lit by a small bed lamp. We see Louis sleeping lightly or resting on the bed. Beside him sits Geneviève. The immediate interior, in semi-darkness, shows a window revealing a darkened sky and the moon whose rays shine dimly into the room, where can be seen a wooden table with two chairs and a modest but comfortable-looking easy chair and simple divan. Suddenly, there is heavy knocking at the outer door from offstage. Persistent. A voice calls:)

Seigneur, seigneur, my lord d'Orléans!

(More knocking and calling. After a few minutes, Louis exits from the bedroom in disarray and goes to the outer door. Before doing so, he leaves the bedroom door ajar where a light is relit. Louis answers and opens the outer door. One of his courtiers and a Breton traveller appear, accompanied by the Englishman, Lord William Hailsham)

LOUIS

Explain to me, Jacques, and pray that your reasons for interrupting my slumber be convincing. As I sent word to you an hour ago, our journey is postponed until tomorrow.

(Silence. Courtier waits. The mood of the squire and his companion is sad, solemn but courteous. Louis senses the gravity. He suddenly straightens up, having immediately shed his anger, and, in gentle but attentive seriousness, asks:)

Jacques, present these gentlemen and tell me now what has happened?

(In the meantime, Geneviève has emerged from the bedroom, straightening and buttoning herself, amused, not in the least embarrassed)

COURTIER, JACQUES

My lord Duke d'Orléans, these foreign gentlemen come from Nantes. They are messengers from François, Duke of Brittany. I have explained to them, sir, that we were. . . *(looking at Geneviève who, in turn, shares an amused glance with Louis)* . . . delayed and would arrive in two days' time for the festival in Rennes and then go on to Nantes. . .

DUKE D'ORLÉANS

Yes. . . *(Waiting for a conclusion from the boy's nervous chatter)*

BRETON TRAVELLER

My lord, the English prince is dead. *(pause, Louis is stunned.)* Young Edward and his brother were slain, only days after the king's death. Lord Hailsham, who brought the news from England to Brittany, accompanies me as a messenger from François. He bids you come swiftly and safely to unequivocally accept the Lady Anne of Brittany, his daughter, in marriage.

DUKE D'ORLÉANS

(slowly) The girl has been promised to all the world, to barons, kings and emperors. *(laughing to himself sadly)* The times we live in. Starvation, plague, war, one child bartered. Another murdered.

(to Hailsham) William, who took the boy's life? Richard of York or. . . or Henry Tudor, of Lancaster?

WILLIAM, LORD HAILSHAM

My young lord Edward was found with his arms around his brother, both throats cut. They had been sent to the Tower by their uncle, Richard Duke of York, in preparation for the new king's coronation, after their father's passing. *(pauses, sitting down in melancholy)* They had been frightened to go. Young Edward had said to me that I must feed his pigeons until his return and watch over his rabbit, which my servant-boy took upon himself to do, as I could not – in the heat of civil war. Upon my last visit, Prince Edward had stared at me, pale and lonely for his dead father. He said to me, pointing to his royal ring, that he was bound to succeed his father's shadow, that he would have hoped to rule continuing King Edward's honour, but that he knew that he would not emerge as a living king from the Tower. He would leave only as a shadow. I scoffed but, as I rose to leave, he bade me feel the coldness of his hand to affirm there was life still in King Edward's son. As I did, and indeed his hand was still warm, his eyes bright and moist, but his pale smile was like the heralding of darkness. *(pause, display of emotion)* My prince. Would that I had stayed to protect the lads!

I had seen Richard hold his nephews and sing to them when their father was away, stroll and gaze upon their play in the king's gardens. His was not a hand who would end such lives. *(pause)* But it is he who rules England now.

DUKE D'ORLÉANS

To my mind, it was Henry. He burns with desire for the English throne and he thus rids himself of rivalry for Anne's hand and control of Brittany. Ah, England's civil wars are beyond us. But Brittany can still be defended. Jacques, prepare the horses for travel immediately. We go directly to Nantes with the gentlemen.

JACQUES

Aye, my lord.

DUKE D'ORLÉANS

(turning to Geneviève) A most pleasant afternoon, madam. My regards to your husband.

(He smiles and bows, and Geneviève laughs as she sees them to the door)

GENEVIÈVE

Surely mourning an English prince can wait till the morrow. *(Louis looks at her disapprovingly.)* Indeed, well, I'll send food and wine to follow you, with special gifts for the Lady Anne. Godspeed, Louis. *(This last phrase is said gently, intimately)*

END OF SCENE III

SCENE IV

(This scene is immediately presented at the end of Scene III, at which time Geneviève sees Duke Louis and the others to the door of her quarters. Still smiling to herself as she turns to face the audience)

GENEVIÈVE

Aye, what a wickedly handsome lad.

(suddenly serious) 'Tis tragic when a child dies. Aye. *(said in sad reflection)* Well, the Duke d'Orléans will now return to give the promised support to François of Brittany and our Lady Anne.

(Geneviève steps forward as the action she describes will take place behind her) There'll be a war, promoted by Landais – you remember – François's treasurer and recently appointed chancellor. Supporters of François and Anne will confront the Breton rebels pushed to revolt by the regency of France. Lords, barons, merchants and peasants of the same land, all Bretons, will confront each other in battle. It will be a most extraordinary battle, called La Guerre Folle – the Insane War. Gui and Dinan commanded the rebel barons and the lord d'Orléans led the defenders of the Duke of Brittany. But when the two forces faced each other on the battlefield, many recognised a relative, a comrade, a friend and not a man would strike another, despite the call to meet in battle, despite Chancellor Landais's urgent appeals to advance and conquer the Breton rebels. Those who had engaged themselves to battle sheathed their swords and grasped the hand of their enemy. There was a murmur, a merging of soul and wrath, so that within the hour they had returned as one united force to the Duke of Brittany's cattle. They stormed the castle in search of their avowed common enemy: Landais; Landais the ambitious favourite of Duke François; Landais, torturer and murderer of

Chauvin; Landais the anglophile minister so hated by the former Spider King and the regents of the underage French king; Landais the supporter of the Tudor rebellion and Henry's accession to the English throne. Storming the castle, this time Landais was found in François's wardrobe. The Duke caressed the brow of his favourite and requested that justice be delivered without taking Landais's life, that he be tried fairly. He could do no more for his minister. François and Anne only heard the maddened cries of the mob and Landais's frightened screams. He was hanged, without trial, justly or unjustly, the chosen scapegoat, the chosen catharsis of Breton wrath. They took his life to unite themselves politically, and that they did. But Duke François was never the same, never as certain, or as strong. *(said with sadness, reflection)* In any case, Breton forces were united behind the Duke, strong enough, or stronger at least when Brittany faced France's declaration of war. The Duke d'Orléans led François's forces. Aid came from Austria, Holland, Italy and Prussia. Shortly after war broke out with France, Charles VIII acceded to the French throne. Battles were lost thereafter and within months King Charles rode into Brittany's cities with his regent sister. In the days following, François lost his second wife, Anne's mother, Marguerite. And his mistress, Antoinette Meignelais; both went with the plague. The tide of the war turned towards defeat for Brittany. Finally, Duke François sent the Prince d'Orange to discuss terms of surrender with King Charles. A week after, François, drained and impotent, ended his life, leaving Anne to fight the last battles of Brittany. Louis, Duke d'Orléans was imprisoned, possibly for life. Poor lad! Yet Anne was not yet conquered as we shall see. Well, we'll take a few moments now to rest your eyes and ears. Our story will proceed thereafter. Right! Now have a rest. I've some shopping to do.

(Geneviève, having put on a cape and taken a basket, opens the door of the quarters. Exits.

Throughout the preceding scene, Geneviève had moved to right downstage while the events of her speech were dramatised without dialogue. The first dramatisation showed two opposing groups of Bretons, their approach and reconciliation. Later, a second dramatisation in the corner shows Chancellor Landais with François and guards watching from the castle – Landais writing out written appeals sent on by messenger from time to time. Then scene with Landais and others with Bretons fades. Lower left and centre stage shows Landais bursting into Marguerite's and François's boudoir and hiding himself in the wardrobe. Breton soldiers come, search and pull him out. Silent acquiescence and words with François. Landais and Bretons leave. Lights fade. Fourth dramatisation centre stage shows Louis reviewing forces. Fifth dramatisation left downstage shows King Charles with the Beaujeux and the Archbishop placing the crown on his head. Lights fade on stage scenes, as they are shown consecutively, while Geneviève remains right downstage, in semi-obscurity. Same area of stage lights up again. King Charles, attired in black, receives the sword of François's emissary who kneels symbolically to Charles. Final scene: right upstage, bedchamber of François. François is lying on his bed. Anne and her sister sit on the bedside. Slowly a priest gives last rites. A doctor and assistant pull the curtain. And Anne lets her head drop while her sister cries. At the same moment, scene of Louis at table, writing, in torn shirt, surveyed by an armed guard)

END OF ACT TWO

Five minute pause during which time musicians play the Breton tune 'Le petit pont'. (11)

ACT THREE

SCENE I

(Decor used in an earlier scene, showing exterior of château from main entrance well in the background. In foreground can be seen the village with the same decor and people from Scene IV, Act One. Slight change in placement of people on stage. Slowly the drawbridge in the distance comes down and Duchess Anne emerges, riding side-saddle, from the château preceded by Philippe Montauban. Within the village, the activity slows and in some cases stops, as people turn, looking towards the Duchess's party. A few people point and excitement increases, as it is realised that the Duchess is coming into Nantes – the village. The Duchess and Philippe proceed very slowly as the people prepare themselves for the entrance. Philippe gallops ahead, crosses the river and dismounts; there is buzzing as the squires arrive carrying several banners bearing Anne's emblem (ermine and cordelier) and hold them high on each side of the passageway.

Duchess Anne arrives and passes through. The villagers bow or incline their head. The children run towards her. In the excited flock there are one or two musicians – one playing a Breton flute, one a bagpipe, producing again first part of Breton tune 'Le petit pont' (12). A group of little girls laugh and, holding hands, hop and play in the circle. A confident Breton peasant steps forward and helps the Duchess Anne to dismount. The Duchess is simply attired in a Breton cape, but she wears her customary headgear and dress underneath. Philippe inclines his head, gives her his arm and leads Anne to the centre of the stage. The young Duchess has a serious, sad but determined demeanour)

ANNE

(Addressing the villagers of Nantes) Merci, Philippe. It is a glorious day to begin a journey. We have fought a war and lost a sovereign; I, a father, Duke François II. I bear his arms, the cordelier of François, next to my own, the ermine paw. The two are bound together, as I am bound to protect our land and our history. In the shadow of my father and his patron saint – the beggar Francis of

Assisi – I come to you, to beg knowledge and faith. I seek to know my people and my country. *(pause)* So I leave you for a time. Guard my father's castle well. Use the cannon and arms he delivered and placed among you only if there should be no other way to protect Brittany. *(Anne prepares to mount)*

A WOMAN IN PEASANT COSTUME, WHOM THE AUDIENCE RECOGNISES AS GENEVIÈVE

What paths will our lady choose?

ANNE

The scroll, Philippe.

(Philippe steps forward to the people and hands the scroll to Duchess Anne who unrolls it and traces her journey)

We move north to La Baule, Le Croisic and Guérande along the coast to Quimper. And then inland in the forest of Paimpont; then north again. We circle the land and then move cross-country to Rennes, to report to our Parliament. I will make a final pilgrimage to Ste Anne d'Auray. Then home again, to Nantes.

(*As the Duchess speaks of her journey, the lights fade. We see only the party of Anne, Philippe and her handmaiden moving slowly around the stage in and out of the dark. Every time they return to a lighted area, their appearance and demeanour differ slightly. They move offstage then return, at which time the lights all come up and the decor is changed to show a small Breton village: small thatched roofs and granite, late medieval towers. Before one tower, there is a small inlay of stone in the form of a circle with a statue roughly carved on the side, in front of which the Duchess Anne is kneeled. She has her back mostly to the spectators, thus at an angle. Some of the Bretons are working a marshy field a little way off, left upstage. Many of them are soaked from the marsh and the early morning rain and their feet and ankles are covered with mud. Lightning is seen in the sky and thunder is heard by all.*)

PHILIPPE

My lady, must we journey in the storm? Within minutes we will be drenched. We have travelled throughout Brittany, built sanctuaries and led pilgrimages; we have supped modestly with the simplest and when the most impoverished had no more than diluted porridge to offer, we ate not well. We shared the discomfort of straw-covered ground when there were no beds. *(pause. Then, in a self-justifying manner)* I do not complain. Living, sleeping and praying was far more difficult in war. To me, the dampness of the earth and an empty stomach are customary strains of battle and duty. But you, my lady, are very young and, with due respect, my Duchess, delicate and precious.

ANNE

I do not follow, Philippe.

PHILIPPE

You are precious to Brittany, my Duchess.

ANNE

Have I not borne sufficiently well the trial of our journey, Philippe?

PHILIPPE

Yes, well, my lady.

ANNE

It was your counsel that encouraged me to move closer to the lives of our people, Philippe. I remember how you took my hand the day my father died and you said, 'Go out and breathe death's passing. History has made you a sovereign. Now go and know those whom you serve. . .' Your counsel serves me well, Philippe, and I am grateful for your protective presence.

PHILIPPE

Aye, I would have disobeyed had my lady not allowed me to accompany her. It would have been too hazardous, and unwise. You are our sovereign, Lady Anne, and *(pause)* paradoxically, because you are so precious, your freedom is diminished by your power. In any case, my lady, we will depart shortly, as you wish and as we planned, so that you may arrive in Rennes to address and report to your Parliament. I bid you, let them see a strong sovereign duchess. I have engaged a carriage so you may arrive with dignity – it is unfortunate, my lady, but human nature is such that the sight of a rain soaked child on horseback will evoke no comprehension of power or authority. One dispassionately attributes weakness and defeat to sensitive, humble persons affecting no grandeur. Therefore, when we travel to Rennes, be seated, poised majestically in a carriage and not stoically sitting upon a tired animal such as this. *(gesturing to the Duchess's horse)* Take out your crown and your ermine cape and wear your finest clothes – not the noble rags you bear among the humble people to whom the simple truth can be spoken. *(pause, then gently)* You have touched them and lived and prayed with them,

Anne. You know each other and that knowledge will help you. Now, return to the world of façades and duplicity. Shed your humility now, my lady, for governing, sadly, bears no relation to compassion. Bear grandeur and power, not emotion, for you have enemies about.

(Anne, in the course of Montauban's speech, turns and sits upon a pile of rock. As Philippe speaks, thunder is heard in the distance and the sky is darkly clouded.)

ANNE

The sky is sombred, Philippe, by the wounded passions of these folk. And yet never have I felt more completely the tempestuous strength of my Celtic race. We have seen in their midst the vestiges of plague, entire families buried in lonely churchyards, beggars with no shelter, not even a fire in the night to warm themselves. And still they dance and sing our Breton legends and smile as each sun rises. You have shown me violence and beauty, feast and famine. From the pardons of Ste Anne d'Auray, to the fishermen of St Malo – the wheat and cabbage fields of the north-east, the mystical forest of Paimpont and the vineyards bordering on the Loire. *(coming to an emotional, breathless climax)* And all the many people and faces and hands bent before me, as if I were their saviour. *(overwhelmed)*

PHILIPPE

(Tenderly, softly) You have ceased, in their eyes, to be no more than a symbol, child. Now, having seen you and heard your voice, your legitimacy is confirmed. And they have more hope.

ANNE

Hope for what, Philippe? Even as their ruler, I cannot change their condition, except to give them a little more bread and a mandate on their own identity. And to keep war out of their lives.

PHILIPPE

That is all they expect and more than most monarchs hope for.

ANNE

They shall have more. *(determinedly)* You will see, Philippe. The night you carried me to safety when the rebels came – you will not regret that. *(nodding in the distance)* There, our carriage arrives.

(A group of Breton peasants arrives to bid farewell to their Duchess and to escort her to her approaching carriage on the other side of the marsh)

ANNE

I will ride to the outskirts of Rennes as I have up to this moment, on horseback *(Philippe protests)*. Then I will do as you advise, Philippe. I will change my attire and my transport and will enter the gates of the Breton Parliament as Lady Anne, Duchess of Brittany.

(Philippe is satisfied. She begins to walk to the left towards offstage, passing the carriage. A young Breton peasant runs after her)

PEASANT

(In a thick Welshlike, Celtic accent) Me lady. 'Tis poorly on the marshes – deep and muddy – and in this season of the rains, you need proper slippers. I have made a solid pair of sabots for you, Lady Anne. Wear them, please, for your protection.

(He bends to Anne's feet and offers to put them on. Anne smiles and puts her feet forward. He puts on the wooden shoes. She bends and touches his hair, smiles and laughs with flashing eyes, clasps the proffered hand of a peasant, waves good-bye and walks upstage towards the carriage, slams shut the opened door, walks towards the horse and mounts, followed by Philippe and Anne's handmaiden. They ride, Anne in the lead, to left offstage. A driver follows with the carriage. The Breton peasants watch, and some run after her, then all return to their work; thunder and lightning strike and one hears the sounds of drizzling rain at the beginning of a storm. The Bretons take notice of it but continue working in the fields steadily)

END OF SCENE I

SCENE II

(Parliament hall in Rennes. On one side of stage we see the dimly-lit figure of the Duchess Anne conferring with magistrates. She appears to be sitting at a table as the gowned men stand around her, a clerk and a cardinal seated on each side of her. She is signing decrees and involved in serious discussion with her magistrates and with Philippe, standing at her side. The audience can hear no more than brief words here and there of their consultation. Entering on forestage from right offstage are Maréchal Rieux and Madame Françoise Dinan.

On right upstage is Alain d'Albret with Pierre Rohan, dimly-lit by the arched window. D'Albret and Rohan are on a higher level than the others. Steps separate their backstage position from that of Rieux and Dinan)

MADAME DINAN

Be still, my friend. Speak softly, so that they hear none of our words. *(pause)* It was not long ago that the child was learning to rhyme and weave under my instruction. It was I who taught her script, poetry and rank. I gave her bearing and elegance. And now, as she assumes her government, I stand in the shadows. *(spoken with bitter irony)*

MARÉCHAL DE RIEUX

There is Montauban *(as Philippe bends to speak silently to the Duchess Anne)* from whom she receives counsel.

ONE OF THE MAGISTRATES FROM GROUP WITH DUCHESS

There must be no tarrying on this devaluation; war has brought the inevitable inflation of currency, madam.

DUCHESS ANNE

I have sent word to Nantes to deliver by convoy a portion of the ducal treasury. . .

(Dinan and Rieux straighten up with attention. Dinan whispers to Rieux)

DINAN

Take careful note, Rieux, of this generosity. . .

DUCHESS ANNE

Hopefully, this will remedy the problem, at least until my tax upon landholders is approved by Parliament.

RIEUX

(speaking also in seemingly low tone) Aye. . . The failure of this convoy to reach Rennes is a great possibility, from which we might benefit. . .

A SECOND MAGISTRATE

I would suggest to my lady that such a tax measure might be unwise, possibly misunderstood as hostile to the lords who have only recently ceased to rebel against you.

DUCHESS ANNE

Surely the welfare of Bretons is a matter beyond petty, political antagonism, Lord Loiret. *(moving to the other matters)* We will have reviewed as well the proposed commercial and penal codes protecting the tradespeople and merchants from fraud. The land distribution measure will be under consideration, the trade protection proposal as well.

CARDINAL

Perhaps, in view of the newly won peace with France and the generosity of English support, we would provide necessary exceptions to this protectionist measure.

DUCHESS ANNE

(Firmly) None, Monseigneur. Our economy is in a state of devastation. Half of our population starves or lives only long enough to pay a few seasons of salt tax. War and plague have drained our country of its vigour and innocence. *(pauses, reflectively)* We are not vengeful towards our enemies. But we *must* strengthen ourselves. *(Philippe nods in approval)* There must be no exception to tax on importation.

(The magistrates and cardinal cough uncomfortably among themselves)

DUCHESS ANNE

And as we speak of protection of our trade, there is the serious question of piracy: murderous attacks by foreign mercenary ships on our merchant vessels. We have the means and skills to protect ourselves. Let us create a military fleet to police our waters, and secure the safety of our coastal trade. There are small shipyards up along the western coast we may expand and support. Baron de

Montauban and I have seen the potential and beginnings of a prosperous national industry and means of defence. We spoke to well-endowed merchants at Brest, *(looks at Philippe briefly)* Port Louis, and Quimper, who would eagerly participate and invest supportively if our Parliament should allocate monies for projects to this end. We may thus create for Brittany a naval fleet of great proportion. We will discuss this in Parliament. *(Arriving at a subject of dissent)* And, most finally, we must suppress the 'tithe' *(shudders and protest from group)* – a most arbitrary, crippling taxation upon the poor. *(Philippe looks worried, uncommitted)* The peasants are our greatest strength. We must protect them.

(As her counsellors consult each other and discuss further with each other in inaudible voices and gesturing, slowly the lights dim upon them and we see only their profiles in stillness. Rieux and Dinan resume their speaking as they walk halfway up the stairs, midway towards d'Albret and Rohan. All four are visible for this scene)

DINAN

What nonsense!

RIEUX

(Smiling and turning finally, to sit down on a bench with cane between his legs and palms clenching it)

You endowed her with almost everything, Françoise, except the most necessary and practical form of self-preservation a sovereign must have – selfishness. But that will come later. *(slight pause)* They all acquire it at one time or another. Meanwhile let us benefit from our lady's uplifted soul. *(looking upwards towards the window and the two men)*

My lords, you are both suitors of our Lady Duchess? *(they each respond proudly, "Aye!")*

DINAN

Duke François, however, had promised marriage to my dear half-brother, Alain d'Albret. *(gesturing to her brother)*

RIEUX

And to me.

ROHAN

And to me too.

RIEUX

(laughs cynically) Ah, yes, François needed alliance with his rebels and what better way to do it than to promise them all the power of succession! What a commodity the Duchess Anne became, bartered to and fro to dilute rebellion! *(laughing and rising to walk downstairs with back to the others and face to the audience)* Well, my lords and lady, it would seem that our greatest interest is in mutual support for the moment. For myself, quite frankly, I have no interest in bedding this girl, whose sanctimonious breast could neither elicit nor satisfy a manly passion. But I will *not* be governed by a child. For myself, the power such a marriage promises can be obtained by other means. Duke François was powerless <u>without</u> our military

force. I captured Nantes in his name *without* his assistance. His daughter would have no greater force to oppose me than did he to assist. *(pause, change of tone to more false amiability) But* I am not a man of warring nature and would seek more reasonable, peaceful means. I would support the suit of either of my lords – whichever one of you has the stronger document and support – quite frankly, for I am a practical man.

(pause, Rieux is evidently waiting to hear from the two lords)

DINAN

Alain has a written promise of marriage.

RIEUX

Have you also, Lord Rohan?

ROHAN

None, my lord.

RIEUX

Then, I would say, it would be of greater benefit to you to support d'Albret's suit, as shall I, and strengthen our complicity. Your reward and vengeance would be in the person of d'Albret who would, naturally, control Anne by marriage and orient government in a direction more suited to our common interests.

ROHAN

(Pause) Aye, my lord. *(spoken in an unwilling manner)*

DINAN

And so we will work together. *(smiling to herself)* I was warned once, years ago, by the Duke d'Orléans never to 'intimidate' Anne, never to impose my will upon her political judgement and never to impose upon her marriage with my brother. In my eyes of course it was not an imposition but an honour for Lady Anne not including the legal right of my brother to whom she had been promised.

RIEUX

How did the Duke d'Orléans know of your intentions, madam?

DINAN

Upon return from riding, a letter I had received from the Regent of France had fallen through the pocket of my cape; my chambermaid had neglected to repair this pocket for which she was severely whipped after my humiliating confrontation with my Lord d'Orléans. In any case, his illiterate squire innocently retrieved the letter and, recognising the Beaujeu seal of the Regency of France, he thought it was meant for Louis d'Orléans, who is the King's cousin. It contained, and therefore revealed to Louis, all the details of our complicity: yours and mine, my lord and our arrangement with the Regent Anne de Beaujeu to control Brittany.

RIEUX

You never told me of this.

DINAN

Ah, I was ashamed, Guillaume. I was not proud that a man younger than myself, though of higher rank, could so intimidate me.

RIEUX

(nonchalantly) Were we denounced?

DINAN

No, but Louis kept that letter and to this day has it in his possession. Yet his blackmail no longer stands. Duke François II is dead. D'Orléans is in the King's prison where he has been for three years now. *(She laughs with the nervous relief she has harboured for a good while. Choking with hatred, she spits out:)* He cannot touch me now and my aim will be accomplished.

D'ALBRET

Let us take Rennes and seize the Parliament and make the Duchess our prisoner.

RIEUX

No, my ageing friend. Let us try legal, insidious means. Parliament meets in two months' time. By that day, we will have sent for and received papal permission and approval for marriage between d'Albret and the Duchess Anne of Brittany. She will be able to refuse neither publicly nor privately the will of God's representative. Meanwhile, let us intercept anonymously Lady Anne's convoy containing the portion of ducal treasure she gives to her government to remedy the inflation of Breton currency. After our seizure, such an aborted economic measure will place our Lady Anne in a most vulnerable position. Then we will see. Open rebellion may not be necessary. Then we will see.

(Lights fade except for the lamp outside the tower window. After a few minutes, the entire stage is lit again and we see the Duchess Anne upper stage in formal dress. Towards downstage we see four rows of magistrates and aristocrats, bishops and priests, merchants and artisans and scholars. Each of the three estates is grouped together. Each side of the stage faces the other. Upper stage, Lady Anne is in the middle, seated royally. At her side is her adviser, Baron Philippe de Montauban, also in formal dress. The familiar figure of Geneviève appears lower left stage)

GENEVIÈVE

Well. . . two months have passed now. . . and the Breton parliamentary session is coming to a close. You see the nobles and magistrates of the First Estate, the cardinals, bishops and priests of the Second Estate and, due to François II's egalitarian insistence, the merchants, doctors and craftsmen of the Third Estate. The Duchess Anne is concluding.

DUCHESS ANNE

(Rising before her throne, a rolled parchment open in her hand) We have given exhausting debate today, my lords, holy fathers and gentlemen. Some questions have been settled. Others require further study and review. We have accepted a suppression of the tithe. The proposal for land reform has been debated but remains unsettled and will be receiving further, hopefully very serious, consideration. You have courageously supported the tax law reforms, the trade protection proposals, measures establishing commercial and penal codes for a consistent yet firm judicial protection of tradespeople from fraud and, finally, you have generously and intelligently supported the need and splendid possibilities for the creation of a Breton navy. You have received as well my report on my journeys and reform measures to be taken up at later meetings. Two months ago I sent word to Nantes to bring to this body a portion of the treasury for protection of our inflated currency. For unknown reasons, the convoy of treasury monies has not yet arrived. *(mutterings of concern and murmurings from parliamentary delegates)* Consequently, I offer to this honourable Parliament my jewels and some additional personal

treasures to ensure the stability of our economy and currency. Whereupon, if there be no further business, I declare 'la séance levée' – the meeting ended.

(Duchess Anne turns to return to her throne and Philippe begins to unroll a parchment to confer with her. A sudden voice is heard calling, "Lady Anne, there is a further matter to consider." Duchess Anne and Philippe turn in surprise towards the orchestra pit from which mounts d'Albret with an emissary from the Pope, followed by Rieux and Dinan. As they reach the top of the stairs, d'Albret continues)

D'ALBRET

The matter of marriage and succession.

(He moves towards the throne where Anne has just sat down, preparing herself for acute opposition. D'Albret's party follows him and they bow to the ground together. Dinan and Rieux move to the left whereas the emissary goes to the right side of d'Albret. D'Albret

is speaking to the Duchess but turns to the Parliament to whom he truly addresses himself)

D'ALBRET

I share with you – honourable lords, priests and gentlemen – a document signed by the Pope Alexander VI, approving and blessing the promised marriage of Duchess Anne of Brittany to Sir Alain d'Albret, a promise made in written form and signed by our late Duke François II and Sir Alain d'Albret, witnessed by her ladyship Françoise Dinan and Monseigneur l'Archevêque. I submit to you, honourable gentlemen and Lady Anne, these documents and await your recognition and blessing.

DUCHESS ANNE

(examines with ironic attention the documents and the humble demeanour of Dinan. Then she speaks quietly and slowly) Gentlemen of Parliament, I do not recognise the claim put forth by Lord d'Albret. I do not recognise: I do not submit. I do not know how,

sir, you persuaded Pope Alexander VI to administer his seal to this document but, I warn you, your suit is based on the testimony of traitors. You, sir, were not among the rebels or the spies whose collaboration with the French regency broke my father's will. Long ago, upon his last visit to Nantes before his capture, the imprisoned Duke d'Orléans gave me a letter. If necessary, I will bring it forth for your perusal and for legal confirmation by our Parliament. It identifies certain royal spies in the ducal palace at Nantes, for it was written by Anne de Beaujeu, former Regent of France. It is in my chambers. And it will remain there, in my possession, until Brittany has no further need of it. *(pause)* Do you still pursue your 'documented request', Lord d'Albret?

(D'Albret slowly lowers his hands. The Duchess Anne steadily stares at him. He takes the documents and tears them up, swings his cape around him, says brusquely, "My lords!" Storms out in angry humiliation. As Dinan and Rieux prepare to follow him, the Duchess calls to them)

DUCHESS ANNE

My lord and lady, transmit to the Lady Regent and her brother King Charles of France my respectful hope for lasting, uncompromising, unspoiled peace.

(Rieux and Dinan, consequently unmasked as spies for France, turn pale and, enraged with humiliation, follow d'Albret and leave)

DUCHESS ANNE

(again repeating) Gentlemen, our session is adjourned.
(The Parliament gets up and leaves with low murmuring)

GENEVIÈVE

(Still in original position lower left stage, unseen and unheard by the others) Well played, my lady.

PHILIPPE DE MONTAUBAN

Does such a letter exist, Duchess?

DUCHESS ANNE

(amused at his perspicacity) It did, sir. Louis gave it to me the night before his military defeat. *(pause)* But it was burned unknowingly by a faithful servant, Geneviève, who, in seeking to protect us all, destroyed papers and correspondence exchanged between Louis and my father. She did not know that this letter was among them.

GENEVIÈVE

(coughs and smiles nervously, comically) A stupid lack of prudence on my part, my lady. *(not heard by Philippe and Duchess Anne, only by the audience)*

PHILIPPE

We were most fortunate, today, Anne.

DUCHESS ANNE

Yes, Philippe, most fortunate indeed.

(The two walk back together backstage. The stage is still lit. Geneviève remains briefly.)

GENEVIÈVE

(a strong, but scatterbrained manner) Well, it's most embarrassing. I've only two hands, you see, and they've got me playing this role and that, filling in the gaps with no time to finish me sweeping. So when you have rebels invading and a audience awaiting, you just can't leave secret papers around for everyone to see, can you now! Ah, well! *(sighing, forgetting her irritation, as Duchess Anne enters.*

Lights around Geneviève go out but she remains in the light and Duchess Anne sits at a dressing table. Geneviève smiles and says, "Ah, there's a love." She comes forward and unbraids the hair that Duchess Anne has just let down. Geneviève starts to laugh wickedly and says)

GENEVIÈVE

Did you not see the look on old d'Albret when my Lady Anne threatened to expose his supporters. . .? Ah, that was most entertaining. . .

(Three ambassadors from Charles appear at the left-hand side of the stage with French breastcoats, hats and parchment, dressed as King Charles's legal emissaries)

ONE OF THE AMBASSADORS

As representatives of King Charles VIII of France, we transmit His Majesty's commands – amendments to the Treaty of Verger.

(Duchess Anne looks towards the audience, as if they were the King's messengers demanding her attention. She regards them with controlled and amused indignation. The ambassadors also face the audience as they speak)

ANOTHER AMBASSADOR

(Unrolling the parchment, reading) Firstly, King Charles assumes the responsibility of guardianship over Lady Anne and Lady Isabeau, the heirs to the duchy of Brittany. Secondly, His Majesty proclaims that Lady Anne must seek the King's authorisation before she assumes the title of Duchess in public ceremony.

A THIRD AMBASSADOR

The Treaty of Guérande ending the Breton Wars of Succession three hundred years ago included the condition that, should the Montfort Duke of Brittany fail to produce a male heir, the rights of succession return to the House of Blois, of which the Lady Penthièvre is the only survivor. Given the point that the late King Louis XI, father to Charles, had purchased from Lady Penthièvre the right to succession, King Charles claims jurisdiction over Brittany and demands that the title of sovereign or duchess be accorded only by his authority.

DUCHESS ANNE

The clause of which you speak, gentlemen, was rejected by the Breton Parliament in power at the time of the Wars of Succession.

(In the course of this encounter, Geneviève supports quietly Lady Anne, standing motionless behind her with supportive and sometimes comic expressions)

THIRD AMBASSADOR

In the King's eyes it is no less valid than Salic Law.

DUCHESS ANNE

Gentlemen, when one speaks of Salic Law, one means the law of the Franks, the law of men. In Brittany, whether our leaders have wombs or testicles, one sex does not use primitive tradition to exclude the other from legitimate succession. *(pausing, waiting a little impatiently)* And your third amendment?

SECOND AMBASSADOR

The King of France demands that all foreign mercenaries who have fought against the crown in the last wars be dismissed and exiled immediately.

DUCHESS ANNE

Is that all?

(The ambassadors look at each other, slightly bewildered)

FIRST AMBASSADOR

Yes, my lady.

DUCHESS ANNE

(pause, aware of the consequences of her answer) Tell His Majesty that I, Duchess of Anne, do not recognise, and neither will the Breton Parliament, consider his amendments.

(The ambassadors are indignant, angry though respectful)

FIRST AMBASSADOR

Lady Anne, the King will not accept a refusal. He is a compassionate man, but your disobedience would bring French hostility and *war*.

DUCHESS ANNE

(with controlled indignation and amusement) My disobedience? You do not fathom to whom you speak, sir. *(First ambassador is slightly shaken but no less condescending and angry. Duchess Anne turns back to her mirror, through which the audience views her reflection, at angle; she concludes:)* Convey to your King my good wishes and my answer. That is all.

(The ambassadors, disorientated and worried, bow)

Ah, yes, and tell King Charles that I am betrothed and married by proxy to the Emperor Maximilian of Austria.

(The ambassadors are stunned and murmur among themselves. Lights upon them fade. Geneviève begins to comb the Lady Anne's thick luxurious hair.)

GENEVIÈVE

It was a bizarre act, my lady, this betrothal and proxy marriage with Maximilian. Who was the old goat who represented him?

DUCHESS ANNE

Wolfgang of Polhaim, his ambassador.

GENEVIÈVE

I was a bit indignant for you, love – how you had to lie on a bed and allow that ugly old man to uncover your leg all the way to the knee and place his leg – only his leg, mind you – next to yours. Thank God the consummation was only symbolic. Wouldn't have been too pleasurable with the hairy old fool. Now, had it been Louis or King Charles or Philippe, a wedding night would be a feast of pleasure. *(smiling and sighing in her fantasies)*

DUCHESS ANNE

(laughing uncontrollably) Stop now, you lusty old woman! Ah, Gen. *(pause)* I asked you once to tell me my future. Now, the wondering is over. I am married and Brittany will be defended by Austria, by an empire. *(change of tone, becomes serious)* But only to you and Louis would I admit that I am overwhelmed and uncertain.

Any further word or change regarding the Duke d'Orléans's condition?

GENEVIÈVE

Nay, my lady, except that he be caged, contained and suspended, but fed enough to live in his own filth.

(Anne looks at Geneviève in disbelief and horror)

GENEVIÈVE

(nodding sadly, bitterly, in reply to Lady Anne) Aye, my lady, the conditions of his prison are not humane. Your pleas for his freedom are of no use. In the Regent Anne's eyes you were not only the inspiration of Lord d'Orléans's rebellion against the crown, you were the Regent's competitor. It is more probable that he be liberated, yet for other reasons. He is the husband of the King's dearly beloved sister, Jeanne, and King Charles may also wish to take advantage of a possible alliance with Louis or his capacity to win you over.

DUCHESS ANNE

Send another messenger to Louis, and *(pause)* bid him know that he is in our thoughts. Tell him of the measures we have taken and that we work for his freedom. *(pause)* And, bid him know that he be no less imprisoned than I.

GENEVIÈVE

(Consoling and in an enigmatic manner) Aye, lady, but the story's not over and will possibly take an unexpected turn.

(A messenger arrives and announces)

MESSENGER

My lady, word has come that Nantes has fallen to the rebels. Rieux and his party control the castle. The south and northern coast are in a state of siege. Lords d'Albret, Rohan and Gui are attacking and occupying your ports with ships and cannon from King Charles.

(Duchess Anne is, of course, shocked and alarmed by this news. Baron Philippe de Montauban enters quickly, before the Duchess Anne has recovered and before she has responded to the messenger)

PHILIPPE

There is further news, from the King of France, my lady.

(He gives her a rolled scroll of parchment)

DUCHESS ANNE

(pause during which she looks intensely and yet steadily and fatalistically at Philippe. She takes the scroll, reads silently. She reads aloud an essential section.) 'And thus the terms of our alliance having been violated, I send arms against the Bretons. Prepare for battle, Lady Anne, and pray that the violent resolution of our differences spares our people from too many months of sacrificial battle and plunder. Declared this day the second of January, the year of our lord 1490.' *(fatalistically)* War once again. Our strength is not yet recovered. Just at a time when we might have fed and protected

every child and person, we must face rebellion and French invasion; just at a moment when Brittany had clasped the keys to its own survival and strength, rebels and ambitious Franks rip us apart once more. *(Duchess Anne recovers from her despair, becomes lucid and uncompromising)* Prepare for a military expedition, Philippe. We should arrive on the morrow if we ride all day. After an evening rest, we, with our knights, shall liberate Nantes. See to it, Philippe.

PHILIPPE

My lady!

(bows in obedience and exits)

END OF SCENE II

SCENE III

(Outside Nantes castle. Duchess Anne and her party, mounted, prepare to cross the drawbridge into the castle. As her knights in the party advance, they call for entrance)

KNIGHT

What ho! *(shouting)* Her ladyship returns to the ducal palace. We bid thee lower the bridge.

(To the puzzlement of the knights, Duchess Anne, her sisters Isabeau and Gabrielle and Baron Philippe de Montauban, there is only silence. Finally Rieux, flanked by two knights, appears at the top of the castle and Dinan is visible through a castle window)

PHILIPPE

My lady!

(points to Rieux and then gestures to Dinan. Duchess Anne looks steadily; without flinching, she swings her horse and guides it sidewise until she reaches the side of the moat closest to the tower. The stage scene has been reconstructed so that although the audience recognises the same bits of scenery used in past scenes of Nantes, the decor is placed differently. In order to convey fully the verbal exchange and

facial expressions, each of the parties faces the audience as if they were facing each other)

RIEUX

Good day to your ladyship. Welcome! We have hoped for your visit.

DUCHESS ANNE

My people await my entrance, Lord Rieux. As your sovereign, I order you to withdraw – or we will enter by force. Lower the drawbridge and we will speak of peace.

(As Duchess Anne finishes speaking, Philippe de Montauban gestures to the emerging forces of well-armed knights around the castle walls and windows. A great number of such men are seen, armed, to support Rieux's occupation of the castle)

RIEUX

My child, look around you. Do you *seriously* wish to propose military occupation? My forces are many, yours are few. Every soul knows that you, dear lady, would not send soldiers to a battle with such a high probability of dying. *(feigning indulgence and compassion)* But I speak of peace with you, Lady Anne. Come forward to speak and I will guarantee your entrance and safe conduct. Lady Dinan and I are most eager to talk with you once again.

DUCHESS ANNE

(sensing a trap) Lower the drawbridge then and we will advance.

RIEUX

Nay, my lady, you must come alone.

PHILIPPE

(fearful of a dangerous trap) Do not, Anne. Once you are within, you will be held against your will and forced to marry d'Albret, while you are completely at the mercy of the rebels and the French.

DUCHESS ANNE

Ah, my Maréchal, you think me a fool! I bid you come forth and meet me on the bridge, neither of us accompanied nor mounted and we shall speak of peace.

RIEUX

Nay, Lady Anne. I will not.

DUCHESS ANNE

Then open the gate of my city and <u>let us enter</u>.

RIEUX

Nay, lady.

DUCHESS ANNE

Let my people leave at least.

RIEUX

Nay, my lady.

(Violently, Duchess Anne swings her horse away from the ducal castle and leads her party away. The castle falls into darkness. Suddenly a servant and merchant encounter the ducal party)

MERCHANT

Duchess Anne *(Bowing, servant scraping ground obsequiously)* I come from Rennes where our people do beseech you to advance for your own protection. We would be greatly honoured to offer your ladyship refuge in our city.

DUCHESS ANNE

I thank you both and all whom you represent. I will indeed, forthwith, hasten to Rennes. *(reflects a moment, consults with Philippe)*

PHILIPPE

Opportunity presents itself, Anne. *(pause)* At this time, your consolidation of power and popularity is critical. Seize the moment and perform the ceremony that will elicit for you much needed immeasurable public support. You have enemies among rebel barons. But, among your people, you are adored.

DUCHESS ANNE

(She looks at Philippe long and hard, and says, with eyes alight) So be it!

PHILIPPE

Kind sirs!

(servant comically looks around to find whom he is addressing in the plural) Tell your people to send for the Archbishop. Tell them that in two days' time the holy coronation of the Lady Duchess of Brittany will be performed in the Cathedral of Saint Pierre before the faithful inhabitants of the city of Rennes. Tell your people. Tell all of Brittany!

(Lights fade. We see Duchess Anne at the centre of the stage bent before an altar. The Archbishop is holding a crown over her head. She is dressed in simple dark blue, with hair flowing luxuriantly upon her shoulders. Her dress is simple – long and fitted to show the slimness of her young figure. A rope, thinly braided, is tied around her waist. Light rests solely upon her)

ARCHBISHOP

Therefore, in the name of God and Brittany, I crown thee Duchess – ruler of our sovereign state.

(The Archbishop places the crown on her head, moves towards her, and hands her the sceptre. She stands and turns to face the audience. A voice is heard to shout: "Vive la Duchesse Anne!" Philippe appears out of the darkness and places the ermine cape on her shoulders. Both the Archbishop and Philippe slip into the darkness and Anne stands alone. Lights intensify on her only)

END OF SCENE III

SCENE IV

(Interior hall of Parliament at Rennes. The Duke Louis d'Orléans sits alone, cape drawn over and around him. He sits in the window, in right upper stage where Rohan and d'Albret were in an earlier scene. It is twilight and sun shines dimly from outside on to him. He is looking outwards. He is thinner, tired. He turns and sees a

dulcimer which he goes to and picks at, slowly, half-singing, half-reciting a song based upon one of the poems written by his father during his own captivity of twenty-five years in England, 'Belle, bonne, non-pareil'. Lady Anne enters as he sings. She stops at the side, climbs the stairs at the left leading to the tower window where Louis is. As she climbs, a young peasant woman followed by a young male peasant enters slowly from lower left and walks more quickly than Anne with a torch to light the candelabras for the coming evening. She is entranced and touched by Louis's recitation to the melody 'Le diable noir' (13). The peasant woman moves and dances expressively to the music. As she moves across the room, she lights the candelabra with her companion's help. They dance together. As they finish dancing and leave the stage, Louis finishes his song and the lower stage is lighted by candles. Anne moves up to Louis, tenderly but with dignity)

DUCHESS ANNE

Louis, *(pause)* . . . my lord d'Orléans.

(Turns, as d'Orléans puts down instrument, stands and bows. As he clasps and kisses her hands warmly, Duchess Anne notices the scar of an old head wound)

DUCHESS ANNE

The wound you received at Saint Aubin still has its scar. *(touching his scalp)* You had assured me in your early letters that your injuries were minor, superficial. But a wound whose mark would remain after three years of imprisonment must have been deep and considerable.

D'ORLÉANS

(Putting his hands on top of hers where the scar is) Oh, that came from a drinking bout. War leaves no physical scar of terrible depth on me. Even loss of freedom – unyielding immobility – only constrains and brutalises the soul but leaves no visible mark, unless one is tortured, which, of course, *I* was not, being of royal blood. *(Emphasis on I to suggest that others were tortured.)* It is passion, romantic love, a whisper of seduction which leaves me weak and bleeding,

marked for life. *(His façade of joking fails to hide unhappiness and truth)*

DUCHESS ANNE

(Looking intensely at Louis, then regaining her composure and appearing solemn)

But you have not come to speak of past sacrifice or to prick our memories with verses we sang in Brittany's finer days before the wars and the plague. . . before my father's last breath.

D'ORLÉANS

(Taking her arm and holding her hand as be leads her downstairs on the right) You're too old for verses, now, Brett. *(smiles)*

DUCHESS ANNE

Never! *(Continues to smile and laugh with him until they reach the main floor)*

D'ORLÉANS

Charles has sent me.

DUCHESS ANNE

(suddenly serious, comprehending) For this reason, your prison doors were opened: you were liberated to play the King's mediator. Your cousin, His Majesty, is finally earning my respect. What better demonstration of generosity, of superior strength and advantage, than to send as one's own emissary the ally of one's enemy.

D'ORLÉANS

You wound me Anne. I remind you that my alliance with Brittany, with your family, was not in defiance of my King, but to the Regency of Anne de Beaujeu and her manipulation of my cousin. By her order I was imprisoned and caged, so like was her rage and brutal power to that of her father's, the Spider King. *(pause)* King Charles rules alone now, thank God, independently. If not for that, and the supplications of my wife and yourself, I should still be imprisoned.

And though I was treated well, life without freedom, Brett, is madness. Well, I do not conceive how my father survived twenty-five years in the Tower of London. His poetry bears no mark of anguish or lonely stoical suffering of the soul; it contains no profound pronouncements of revolt or self-denial. Instead he gave the world the most joyful verses filled with grace and simple pleasures. 'Tis as if he had come to love his cage. *(bitter, after a pause)* Not I. *(closing his eyes remembering the torment of imprisonment)* Not I.

DUCHESS ANNE

(pausing, then repressing her emotion, becoming businesslike) What terms do you offer me, my friend?

D'ORLÉANS

The most binding and the most definitive. Marriage to the King of France.

DUCHESS ANNE

(laughing heartily from amazement and irony.) My lord d'Orléans, I have slipped away from the most greedy and lascivious of would-be husbands who could not bed me. I was engaged to both the heir and the pretender to the English throne. Numerous Breton barons, viscounts and counts have courted me and many claimed to have been promised my hand by my father. Except for Edward, silenced before he came of age, I have slipped away from them all. *(The Duchess begins to pour wine for herself and drinks it quickly, glass after glass, in agitation)* I *chose* my husband, the Emperor of Austria; the Emperor Maximilian's support stood Brittany in good stead until your King mused and calculated his distraction by Flemish and Swiss rebellions.

D'ORLÉANS

It is exactly this that Charles's father, the Spider King, did before when the Duke of Burgundy – your father's most willing and powerful ally – was vanquished by Swiss mercenaries. Louis XI, the Spider

King, had bribed them to rebel, to destroy your father's greatest ally. In a strange twist of history, Maximilian of Austria, son of your father's vanquished ally, fails to protect you, again because of Swiss mercenary rebellion provoked by the French King. *(pause)* You did not guard Brittany against a recurrence of history. That is unlike you, Anne, *(pause)* but you escaped d'Albret's clutches and the trap that Rieux and Dinan had set for you – that was an intelligent and most natural manoeuvre – your coronation, my lady.

DUCHESS ANNE

(pauses, absorbing and reflecting, circumspect) Yes. At least for a while, it united my people and brought the rebel barons back into the fold. *(pauses, gives d'Orléans a glass of wine and pours more for herself)* Ah, but it cost me Nantes. I should have foreseen d'Albret's treachery. After the coronation, the rebels came back to support me. I foolishly gave command of my beloved city to d'Albret, as appeasement. Philippe had advised me not to give so much so soon. *(pause)* But the Breton people were wearied and sickened *(pause)* by grim, unending wars and I felt that I must trust the rebels' truce for

their sake. *(determinedly, with intensity)* I needed strong military leaders to protect our stronghold from the French. But d'Albret had never forgiven my refusal of marriage, nor the public humiliation in Rennes.

D'ORLÉANS

And thus did he hand to King Charles the keys to the city of Nantes, your finest and strongest asset; thus had your father by promising your hand to everyone in God's world to secure military alliance; thus had my beloved friend, François II, unknowingly planted the seeds of rebellion and betrayal.

(Duchess Anne, wounded by the truth of d'Orléans's words, looks back at him and pours more wine for him and herself)

D'ORLÉANS

But you have ruled well, my lady. No one could have done more for your people and for Brittany's survival.

(Duchess Anne and Louis are sitting on the steps, both a bit tipsy. Sudden noise of church bells, ringing the hour)

DUCHESS ANNE

(rising, goes to table, puts down glass and looks out of the window. She pauses) It's six o'clock. Time for vespers. You hear the call of Saint Pierre where I was crowned? The priest who climbs to the tower to work the bells *(pointing to the tower)* gives me confession and has each evening service of the last few months recited the same verses telling of the Exodus, of famine and exile. Each evening I used to sit by the altar and see the vacant-eyed youngsters open their mouths to receive communion and the humblest of families inclined in prayer, beseeching the Lord and me to moisten their soil, to end the famine and the plunder and the mysterious glory of battle. Each evening the priest climbs to the tower to bid us come to prayer. I can no longer face the starving faces of my people nor their unhappy supplication to both God and myself because we, God and I, have failed. *(pause, drinks two more glasses of wine, pours Louis another)*

So I no longer pray with the people at vespers *(unemotional, ironic)*. I feel unworthy, too shamed to be in their midst. Thus the priest who climbs the tower to ring the bells of Saint Pierre where I was crowned no longer expects me, and I pray alone. Afterwards, late evenings, before retiring – after his flock has left and he has locked up the beautiful cathedral of Saint Pierre, after he has locked up the echoes and shadows of beseechment and deliverance – afterwards, he comes and hears my confession. And even then, *(pauses, head lowers)* I am not cleansed. They look to me for food, justice and salvation. But I have empty hands. . .

D'ORLÉANS

(Slowly, then peering into the Duchess's face) Only in rare instances do rulers admit they are not gods. A strong ruler speaks of it, to the most loyal and intimate advisers. But *never* to the people. Absolutely *never*. *(pause)* Come now, Anne – if you marry the King, war ends, there is less suffering for everyone.

DUCHESS ANNE

What protection, what guarantees will I have for the sovereignty of Brittany?

D'ORLÉANS

Sovereignty, Anne. A moment past, you were a ruler consumed by guilt for the hunger of your subjects and now you hesitate for a question of autonomy and pride. Nay, I understand, my lady; it is my impatience and fatigue that turns my tongue unkindly. *(pause)* Yes, there are considerable guarantees and *only for that* you marry Charles. You will retain your title. *(seeing Duchess Anne's reaction)* Yes, a title is not enough, I agree. But Brittany will be officially your responsibility. Annexed and held by France and ultimately subject to French law, but relatively autonomous and primarily under your authority.

DUCHESS ANNE

Relatively autonomous? Primarily under my authority? You qualify every advantage you offer me.

D'ORLÉANS

That is the function of a diplomat. Nay, Anne, what choice is better for your homeland? You would not have Brittany portioned up piecemeal by the rebels faithful to Charles, which would happen should you refuse this agreement; for Brittany, now, my lady, is too weak, too shattered to stand again against France. Your English allies have been bought off and defeated. The Emperor is busy with Swiss rebellion and will not be here for a time; at least as Queen, and as the marriage contract and terms of peace would assure you, Brittany would be *intact* and protected by *your own authority*. *(pause)* My lady, I do not relish the thought of losing you again; *(Duchess Anne turns her head, to hide emotional flush)* yet my cousin is a sensitive man, perhaps a bit too awkward and ambitious. But he is worthy of your affection and fidelity. He would honour you *and* Brittany. My advice, my lady, is – marry King Charles.

DUCHESS ANNE

(Reflects, and the bells ring again, six times. When they cease to ring, Duchess Anne turns, pauses, and then says slowly, reluctantly to Louis) So be it. Let the contract be prepared and if the guarantee for Brittany should be clearly stated, I will surrender, unequivocally, to the King. *(turns to d'Orléans)* I am glad you are free, Louis.

D'ORLÉANS

We are never free, my lady, never absolutely.

(kisses her hand, bows, exits. Duchess Anne remains, looks at a painting of her father, picks up wine glass and toasts)

ANNE

To Brittany!

As scene ends, audience hears again the song 'En amour n'a si non bien!' (14)

END OF ACT THREE

Intermission of fifteen minutes

ACT FOUR

SCENE I

(Rome. Interior of Farnese palace. Darkened slightly. We see magistrates, priests and servants walking through and an occasional servant woman or man trailing an aristocratic litter. Around the proscenium stage are galleries ornately decorated with rich lattice-worked balconies and arches. The arched galleries are lit slightly so as to evoke the romance and aura of indefinable danger and mystery of the Roman court. Slowly the stage empties entirely and a young troubadour appears on the corner of the gallery with a lute-like instrument. He begins to sing the provocative deep melody called 'Diable noir' (15). As he sings, a figure appears from the shadows on the same gallery, emerging from behind a column on left upper stage. As he moves from behind the arched-supporting pillars we see only his back. He walks along the gallery away from us, his back to us still. The troubadour continues to sing. As the figure turns perpendicular,

his face is hidden by the shadows and his wide-brimmed hat and scarf. He bears the black robe of a religious man but his bearing is that of a creature filled with tension and ambition, both emotions subdued but obviously unsatisfied. The audience will learn later in the scene that this disguised holy man is Cesare Borgia, the second son of Pope Alexander VI. He has come on a mission of secret discovery, diplomacy on behalf of his father. He descends the stairs slowly, careful to show none of his features nor to face the audience. The troubadour is still singing. As the robed figure reaches the first gallery level, he descends the stairs to the stage, directly facing the audience; as he does so, the lights on the back stage come up and those around the galleries fade in such a way that the arches and balconies and the figure of the troubadour are profiled in shadows against the barely lit background. The troubadour's song fades as well, until only silence and the shadow of arches, columns and balconies surround the robed man centre stage. The man is surrounded as well by slight lighting. As he reaches centre stage and comes to a halt, he slowly raises his head. We see his features –

attractive but intense and cruel. The lights show suddenly another figure, standing behind, away from Borgia, robed also in the shadows)

BORGIA

(without turning) Your master?

FIGURE

My uncle, sir. *(said as a respectful, submissive correction)* He awaits Charles.

BORGIA

(mocking disbelief) The Regent of Milan, Ludovico Sforza, awaits the Valois boy-king, the modern-day Hannibal of France. Sforza, the Moor, awaits invasion and defeat by a power less worthy than all Italy's city states together. And you, Gian Galeazzo Sforza, rightful King of Milan, do you enjoy watching your regent uncle open the doors of Italy to French conquest? Not only does he place the keys of

your city state into Charles's grasping palms but Ludovico brings all of Italy to its knees.

GIAN GALEAZZO SFORZA

(Gian Galeazzo moves forward and turns at an angle towards Borgia. His back is mostly turned towards the audience. His face is almost entirely in the shadows)

Ludovico has seized much of my family's power in Milan. He beckons to the green-eyed French prince to conquer Italy, to liberate its people from the tyrannical families of Sforza, de Medici, Aragon and Alexander. *Alexander VI,* his Holy Eminence, ruling pope of the Vatican City. *(pause, and then, ironically)* Your father, Lord Borgia.

(Suddenly a voice is heard as the lights show three other figures upstage right and left, halfway behind Borgia, at an angle, half-immersed in shadow. The figures are Pietro de Medici, Alexander VI, and Ludovico Sforza, the Moor. The voice heard is that of Ludovico Sforza)

LUDOVICO SFORZA

Cesare Borgia.

BORGIA

Ludovico Sforza. . .

ALEXANDER VI

Ah, we are all present. Good afternoon, my friends. Please forgive the lugubrious site of our meeting. In view of certain political considerations and so as not to arouse panic or rebellion among citizens of our respective city-states, such secrecy is essential. There are five of us present: the Prince, and the Regent of Milan – my lords – *(said as polite greeting)* Prince of Florence, Pietro de Medici, Duke Cesare Borgia and myself – Alexander of Rome, the Holy City. We are here, my friends, to decide upon and prepare for our mutual defence against the power of France. *(pause)* The question is: are we united?

PIETRO DE MEDICI

Where stands Aragon?

BORGIA

Which house of Aragon do you summon? The King of Spain or the Neapolitan bastards?

PIETRO DE MEDICI

Both or either. They control eastern Italy, and, as I understand, are in close association with our young Milano prince, *(gestures to Galeazzo)* Galeazzo Sforza. *(looking around)* As we stand, without them, we will trip and fall before the French arrive. We are only less than half of Italy. Our people threaten revolution. We each carry within our states the force of iron and blood. But we are weak, Holy Father, *weak without the House of Aragon.*

ALEXANDER

Aye, Pietro. *Officially*, Ferdinand of Aragon has opposed our family's power for many years. We are the impure descendants of the Catholic nations which desecrate the city of God. But, in fact, they have tolerated our presence with ease. We have enjoyed considerable intimacy politically and socially. *(Pope Alexander looks desirously at a young woman standing nearby, a courtesan)* Cesare and Lucrezia, my godchildren, *(perceptive glance exchanged among Galeazzo Sforza, Ludovico Sforza and Pietro Medici)* were raised by the Spanish Duke Mendoza of Cordoba.

CESARE

The Duke was the first among soldiers. He taught me swordsmanship and nurtured every manly instinct and talent within me. With him, I identified passionately. There was no greater military mind. No soul more comprehending of my own.

(Borgia's hard, cruel features are touched, paradoxically, for a moment by the wistful memory of his hero's kindness)

ALEXANDER

Yes, unfortunately, his demise was a necessary expediency, as I explained to Cesare, who came to understand his duty, despite his obvious affection for the Duke. But it was a peaceful death.

(Alexander places his hand on Cesare's shoulder, showing consolation and paternal warmth while nonchalantly exposing his own unscrupulous nature)

LUDOVICO SFORZA

One of the first of the Borgias' poisonings, God help us!

BORGIA

(Looking at Sforza steadily with terrifying hate) But not the last. I slew my sister's Spanish lover as I do all those who disgrace or betray my family.

LUDOVICO

(to Galeazzo) These are the kind with whom you wish to lie, my nephew. Would that I could save you from them; I leave you now. *(as Borgia and the surrounding guards emerge from the darkness)* Restrain me not for, as Galeazzo knows, if I die, this palace will be besieged by flame and sword and you will perish in Roman cinders. The Farnese and Borgian guards are no match for Milano marksmen.

(Alexander looks at Borgia and shakes his head in a brief negative sign. Borgia bitterly waves away the guards)

LUDOVICO

(again to Galeazzo) Though we have come to enmity, I bid you – drink not with these men. They will poison you.

(Ludovico leaves. Galeazzo leaves also, moments later.)

ALEXANDER

(slowly) Alas, Pietro, we stand alone against the French. *(pause, wearily)* Do we stand together?

PIETRO DE MEDICI

(pause) Should we have been united? If Castile or Aragon or Austria had joined us, *perhaps* Firenze and the de Medici would have *overcome* their revulsion to your family. *(pause)* But now, there is no purpose. Alexander and Cesare Borgia offer Pietro de Medici no real protection from France nor from enemies within. *(pause)* No, you are cunning, Alexander. You will survive conquest, but I will not emerge from war, bleeding from your knife in my stomach. Arrivederci, *(sarcastic) Holy Father. (exits)*

(The Pope and Borgia are now alone. Geneviève reveals herself as one of the silent women in the shadows as these two appear to converse silently upstage in subdued light. Geneviève is dressed as the

courtesan upon whom Alexander has, and continues to, cast desiring glances despite his anger and fear of the political situation)

GENEVIÈVE

Arrivederci, Pietro! *(looking at the audience. She is upstage and removes her veil)* I must hurry, as Alexander— *(said with affectionate indulgence and familiarity, then correcting herself and using a more formal title)* that is, his Holy Eminence the Pope, wishes me to consult with him *(pause)* in his chambers. *(pause. Fans herself with a black Venetian fan.)* It is February 1492. The Italian princes have discovered, through diplomatic wrangling and spies strategically placed within the court of Charles VIII, that within a month the King of France will begin the invasion of Italy with the most powerful military force assembled since the Crusades. His claim: his great-grandfather Louis II, as an Angevin, ruled over Naples and Charles thereby reclaims his birthright. Charles was *invited* to invade by a group of Neapolitan nobles who had revolted against their rulers, the House of Aragon. Yes, *(laughing)* the Spanish crown. So. . . you can well see that, when the Parliament of Paris approved their King's claims and when Ludovico Sforza overthrew his little nephew, Galeazzo, and urged Charles into Milan, well, it was a wonderful, exciting adventure for King Charles who had dreamed of reliving the expeditions of Hannibal; Charles wanted to emulate the military glory of Charlemagne. He wanted it for France – and he wanted it for himself. *(pause)* Well, the doors are opened now.

(Geneviève begins to move off coquettishly in response to Alexander's entreaties. Then she stops in her tracks all at once and turns around, as if to justify the play's seeming digression)

GENEVIÈVE

Ah, but this play *is* about *Anne of Brittany*, you say. You see, all of this is important; it is all deeply related, I assure you.

END OF SCENE I

SCENE II

(Immediately following Scene I. Geneviève remains standing where she had been. Scene on stage left lights up, shows the French court: Queen Anne of Brittany with her demoiselles, weaving, praying and painting)

GENEVIÈVE

Anne is now the Queen of France, having married Charles some months ago. Thank God the Breton war ended with the marriage, when the Duchess Anne bound her family and its ermine arms to the French crown. And, for a time, despite the transformation of Duchess to Queen, for a time, Brittany was safe. Charles had guaranteed his Queen sovereignty over her own province which remained self-governing. But Anne was bound by their marriage contract to marry Charles's successor, if Charles should die, because well, France had promised Anne and her family continued control over Brittany and, well, the only way for France to control Brittany was to try to control Anne. It's all very tricky, you see. *(nods with pleasure to the scene on the left)* There is my lady Duchess, now with child. As you see, she has transformed the French court. Lady Anne instructed and elevated her court in the arts, religion and morality. She has virtually displaced the brutal ignorance of prior regimes and brought to the French court an artistic and moral renaissance. *(pause)* Look, there with her is Jean Marot, the poet . . . and beside her, the artist Jean-Lemaire le Belge. The Queen peruses the famous 'Book of Hours', written and painted from scenes of Lady Anne's court and kingdom. Ah, my lady. . .

(At this point the stage lights come up further and show the rest of the interior of the French palace at Amboise, in the Queen's chambers. Borgia, Pope Alexander, the Italian court and Geneviève have disappeared. We see Anne with very young women around her, members of the order she created, La Cordelière. A vivacious young man is sitting at her side, speaking to her and sharing with her manuscripts, drawings of his work. Anne listens as well to the recitation of verses (original verses) by Jean Marot, accompanied by his son, Clément. She has in her hand 'The Book of Hours', written in

her honour. *In front of her is a small loom and an unfinished tapestry. The Queen is perhaps unnoticeably pregnant, a month along)*

CLÉMENT

(A small boy, he has just completed the recital of a poem)

QUEEN ANNE

A good verse, Marot. Your son recites your rhyme well. Does he follow your example in poetical inspiration?

JEAN MAROT

The verses he recites, Your Majesty, are his own.

(The young Queen, impressed, and with particular joy, touches her abdomen where a child awaits birth)

QUEEN ANNE

Come here, lad *(touching and looking intently at Clément)*. You were born with genius and creative spirit. Would that I might impart such a legacy to my child. I will bring forth a life in December when all others shun the illusion of heaven. *(with renewed assurance)* The sunlight will shield my infant from the plague, from the germs of cholera and the pox. But life contains more than physical threats. How will he survive the emptiness of power, the fear of lovelessness and lonely mortality? *(pause)* He is a boy – an heir, a duke, a prince. All these things and none *(actress underlines the dichotomy of the previous terms)* for he is as yet only a seed growing large and painfully swelling my belly. *(pause and shared amusement with Marot)*

He will be called Orlando: as Ariosto so named the Emperor of the Franks, so do I the future protector of the Celts. He will be tall and noble. He will be strong and forgiving. He will love poetry, song and laughter – and his love of God will be a love of mercy, compassion and beauty. But how shall I impart to him the hopes subdued in myself, the realised ideal of a just land, ruled only by the laws of humanity and creative genius?

JEAN MAROT

Your Majesty. *(shorter pause)* There is a threshold beyond which one's greatest mercy to oneself and others is to restrain one's former dreams. *(pause)* My son writes verses with meaning. And he believes in the ultimate elimination of suffering and evil. But he is a child and children have a moral vision that ageing weakens along with the bones. For some rare blighters, it remains and sustains the life of a soul clinging to its deteriorating body; and in some rarer cases, the simplistic morality of one's childhood nourishes the soul and grows and grows until it defies death.

(Laughter of Clément who plays blind man's buff with the demoiselles and is being spun around with increasing speed. The attention of the poet and Queen Anne is drawn to the group. And they smile – indulgent, yet fascinated)

JEAN MAROT

(continues) I, my lady, in my youth wrote of the Spider King's prisons, the long sadistic torture, the suspended iron cages which held destroyed and wasted souls praying for an end. *(pause)* That was many years ago. You, my lady, were still a child under the tutelage of your father. Since then I have come to prefer the co-existence of good and evil, of compassion and cruelty. Without one, I would not distinguish the other. And I have felt more keenly the caress of my wife, the warmth and freshness of burning autumn and the monsoons of summer. I believe in simple *life*, my lady; I would not bequeath to my child an insatiable passion, however noble, however heroic. I would that Clément live simply and justly, suppressing no feeling or pleasure.

QUEEN ANNE

(intently following the poet's thought but disturbed by the amorality of his remarks) Nay, but nay, my friend. The greatest gift to one's child is truth and noble purpose. . .

JEAN MAROT

My lady, the two are incompatible. A saint breathes morality but knows not to savour the essence of life, for such a being knows no sin. Cruelty and suffering will never end as long as one rules another. *(short pause)* And *that*, God help us, will always be either by government, by trade or by faith.

(Queen Anne is bewildered at first at his remarks, and stares at him, smiling with sad but disbelieving eyes)

QUEEN ANNE

Send me your child poet, Monsieur.

(The child is brought)

QUEEN ANNE

Write me a poem, Clément, to read to my boy on my pilgrimages to Brittany, so that my firstborn may return to the Celts their freedom and life. Write this poem for me, Clément, as one idealist to another.

CLÉMENT

Yes, my lady.

(Suddenly, there is a buzzing of voices among the women. And then a hush. Geneviève enters running, dressed as a chambermaid. She runs to Anne and quickly curtseys, bows her head and kneels)

GENEVIÈVE

Lady Anne, His Majesty, the King.

(Queen Anne rises carefully. A valet and a courtier enter, bow and stand to the side, expectantly facing the audience. King Charles VIII enters. The demoiselles, the poet and his son kneel in bowed position.

Anne courteously bows her head and curtseys as he enters. Then she resumes a standing position. Charles takes her arm and leads her forward, away from the others)

CHARLES VIII

You are a taskmaster, Anne. It is a spectacle indeed to see the daughters of Europe's most distinguished nobility fabricating cloth and praying, labouring most seriously alongside the daughters of our peasants, merchants and courtesans.

(Queen Anne nods to one of them, who abandons her embroidery, takes up a lute and begins the tune 'Mi ut re ut' (16). Another, following a gesture of approval from the Queen, closes her loom and moves to the corner where she kneels, clasps her hands and prays in front of a painting of Ste Anne d'Auray and a small cross of granite. Another young woman opens a book and quietly recites to some of the women as Clément watches the movement of the tapestry-making and looms. One woman rises and then begins to dance slowly,

irrepressibly and eventually urging a quicker, tempestuously joyful tune from the lute. Queen Anne disapprovingly calls sharply at her)

QUEEN ANNE

Régine!

(The young woman abruptly stops dancing. Her face is suddenly pale and frightened. The music returns to the formerly slow tone. Queen Anne is shaken by her own severity. King Charles looks away, embarrassed by the spectacle of Queen Anne's Puritanism. All of the scene except for Queen Anne and King Charles falls into vaguer, slighter lighting in order to highlight the couple)

CHARLES VIII

This order of ladies-in-waiting is a most unusual egalitarian measure. I understand that you arrange not only their marriages to prosperous aristocrats but you organise as well their education in the arts and morality. . . You even teach them Latin in your leisure hours. That is much to ask of a woman. . . *(laughing)*

QUEEN ANNE

I hope my son will be as quick and intellectually gifted as the young women under my protection.

CHARLES VIII

(King Charles smarts at this remark but retains his cheerful demeanour) Our son, mean you not, Anne? *(He looks somewhat sad, remembering the approaching separation)*

QUEEN ANNE

Forgive me, Charles. *(she extends her hand which he kisses)*

KING CHARLES

(reflectively and shyly) It has been a year of happiness since we wed, a year since we ended our war against each other. The months of intimacy have been blissful, but brief. *(revealing discontent and slight resentment in this last phrase)*

QUEEN ANNE

(embarrassed, pretending ignorance) You leave at dawn, my lord?

CHARLES VIII

(with aroused but tender passion) Aye, my lady, Ludovico Sforza awaits our forces in Milan. Then Florence, Naples, Venice and finally Rome. Would that my great grandfather Louis II, Duke d'Anjou, conqueror and King of Naples and Sicily, could witness the resumption of French Angevin authority in the Italian city states. And so may we deliver the land of infidels.

QUEEN ANNE

(surprised and disturbed) Charles, the French are no better Catholics than the Italians. We may have had our own popes in Avignon two hundred years ago, but the fact remains that the centre of Christian life in our times *is* in Rome.

CHARLES VIII

Exactly the reason that we must preserve its sanctity from the Borgias and the de Medicis: decadent, murdering pigs!

(Suddenly King Charles waves the others away. The lights go off completely on back upper stage and only Anne and Charles are seen. Charles pulls Anne to him, has her sit with him in the wide chair. He places his arm around her. He kisses her passionately. She responds, passive but shaken by her own pleasure and desire. He moves his hands up and down her waist, breasts and hips, rips off her headpiece, pulls apart her bodice, leaving exposed her shoulders and back. He kisses her and undoes her hair. Then, in one impulse, he gathers her

up and swings her over to the bed, surrounded by silk curtains. As he carries her, he enfolds her tenderly in his cape, Throughout the scene Anne is disturbed and frightened by her passion but inflamed with longing and desire as well. Charles kneels by Anne, who is stretched out before him, and places his head and hands on her belly)

CHARLES VIII

(His hands and head still on Queen Anne's abdomen) Early days as yet. Until we meet in Lyon in eight months' time. Send me news of each murmur, of each kick and each pain.

(Charles removes his breechcoat and moves towards her. Anne sits up, Charles's cape wrapped about her)

I desire you, my lady. *(stops, disturbed)* Your cheeks burn, Anne. Always, when I make love to you, your figure reddens like a flame. I pray that it be passion.

QUEEN ANNE

(voice trembling, nervous) My desire is to please you, Charles. But our child. . .

CHARLES VIII

There is no danger.

(He lays her down after pulling the cape from her shoulders)

Until dawn will I lie with you, my Queen.

(Lights fade)

END OF SCENE II

SCENE III

(Lights come up a minute or two later. Queen Anne is seen wearing a white simple robe, tied at the waist. It is dark around her except for a chair, a bed, a table and a french window opening on to the audience area. The stage is carefully lit to make it seem as if the early morning light comes in from the audience. We see her waving

as lights come up, modestly, clutching her robe more tightly closed and wrapped around her. She is far more advanced in her pregnancy. She waves through the window, leaning on the balcony edge, facing the audience, smiling with encouragement and determined assurance as a secondary expedition leaves Amboise; the sound of cheering, horses, armour, orders being given and trumpets. Geneviève appears again carrying drink and food on a tray from offstage. She enters and places the tray on the table by the chair and stands a little behind)

QUEEN ANNE

(without turning to her) It was a long journey for His Majesty. Eight months he has been in Italy. Conquest after conquest. All preceded by revolutions. Charles has been welcomed everywhere in Italy as a liberator. *(Anne expresses surprise as she speaks)* Now we send him reinforcements. I had wished that the King not consecrate himself to this Italian expedition. I had attempted to dissuade him from reclaiming a dead and dangerous heritage. Would that this legacy had not exposed him to what may be a vengeful machination of Alexander and Borgia. Ludovico Sforza of Milan uses my husband to

rule Milan until he turns his back upon him; Pietro de Medici loses power in Florence and suddenly befriends the French King, to entreat him not to invade and thereby topple the Medici family dictatorship. I say, Geneviève, I was and am in profound opposition to my husband's Italian project. But I am only the Queen. My rank has been diminished, Geneviève. As Duchess I was of less importance but wielded greater authority and power. As Queen, I am a figurehead with nothing to say, no right to question, and a husband who seeks glory far from my presence.

GENEVIÈVE

Oh, my lady, consider what education you have brought to his court. You have transformed the mores of an ignorant, illiterate sex. You have taught young women of the people and of noble blood; you have given them instruction, knowledge, and because of you, they know the beauty of the soul and mind. The King – forgive me, my lady – does little good in Italy and history may give him greater glory; but you, Your Majesty, you have done far more to better this country.

QUEEN ANNE

Do you know, Geneviève, they welcomed King Charles in Milan and Florence with wild frantic cheering and dancing. In Venice, Naples, there were thunderous ringing of bells and happy, excited crowds. During the night, blazing torches were carried to light his way into Rome. Everywhere, Charles has been welcomed and exalted as the liberator. *(becomes excited and feverish)* Revolutions occur and city state governments fall wherever Charles moves, as if my lord carried with him a messianic promise. *(excitement subsides and the Queen conveys fatigue and gentle concern)* I am glad for the King. Beyond his own boyish emulation of Hannibal's march into Italy and the legend of Charlemagne's mystical mission to the Holy Land... Oh, how many verses he read and reread to me of Ariosto's *Orlando Furioso*. For that reason, our firstborn will be named Charles Orlando. Beyond the mythical glory the King has achieved for himself and for France, perhaps he has given a measure of liberation and unity to a divided, corrupt land. But, as the former leader of a supposedly conquered people, I do with some experience fear for Charles. I fear that adulation might become discontent, which the

King's allies may use against him. Already Charles has let his head be turned by the favours and compliments they, his former enemies, bestow upon him.

GENEVIÈVE

Aye, my lady.

QUEEN ANNE

We will meet in Lyon next month. To give my husband respite from war. He wishes it.

GENEVIÈVE

Yes, my lady, I suppose one has to be interested to do it. *(looking concernedly at Anne who begins to grimace from pain)* Taking life is far easier than giving it. *(Anne doubles up with pain)*

QUEEN ANNE

Gen, it's time. I can feel it. His little body is bursting my insides. *(She starts to crumple to the ground. Geneviève catches her, holds her, wipes her brow with her apron)* Wait, help me, hold me, Gen. *(she attempts to wave the banner of France's fleur-de-lys embracing the Breton ermine arms.)* The Breton and French knights must have our blessing of solidarity before they leave.

GENEVIÈVE

Oh, my lord in heaven, child, national glory will have to wait. Help little Orlando to come forth. Then your little Celtic King will wave all the banners and play all the trumpets you wish. . .

QUEEN ANNE

Gen, please. . .

GENEVIÈVE

Yes, very well, my lady.

(Queen Anne lifts herself with Geneviève's help and, leaning over the balcony, smiles and waves the banner of their united arms to the audience, the imagined reinforcements)

QUEEN ANNE

Thus, my King and my people, I send to you the breeze of victory of our united arms. I beseech you, be victorious, find the glory you seek and return safely *(wincing with pain)* to your heir. Au revoir – in a month's time, in Lyon.

(Waving anxiously, finally she can sustain the pretence no more, turns her back to the audience and, as the balcony curtains are drawn by Geneviève, she hollers her pain and falls to the ground. The bed on to which Geneviève helps her is behind the balcony window with the drawn curtains. The audience hears her continued cries and

Geneviève's comforting voice encouraging and helping her to give birth. Shadows of a female lying and pushing upon herself as a woman does during childbirth, of Geneviève helping to receive the child and one or other young maids to attend them both can all be distinguished. This continues only for a minute or two. Suddenly the stage falls into darkness. Then a child's cry is heard. Geneviève emerges from the curtain, sweating, exhausted, wiping her blood-stained hands on her apron. She smiles – supremely happy – and curtseys, addressing the audience as she would a person)

GENEVIÈVE

My lord, Your Majesty, you have an heir: a boy, healthy, lovely, endowed with tremendous lungs. My lady Anne is weak but happy and doing quite well. You've a boy, my lord, God bless you. *(tears in her eyes, very moved.*

Geneviève hurries back behind the curtain of the balcony. Lights down)

END OF SCENE III

SCENE IV

(On left stage we see Queen Anne seated in a chamber, reading a letter. On right, the curtains of the balcony are open. Sunshine appears to be shining in. A neatly-kept chamber with a baby's cradle being rocked by a chambermaid can be seen. Geneviève also appears and moves from around the room to her previous position in front of the balcony window. She, through her speech and facial and physical gesturing, announces what Anne is reading in her letter. Geneviève has a towel on her where she has been feeding the baby his milk and probably burping him. She uses the towel to wipe her brow and hands while speaking)

GENEVIÈVE

Well, my lady. I do envy your excitement of seeing the south, of being in Lyon for the last few months. Your lad's very well. Drinking his milk and smiling and laughing, bubbly and sweet when he's got his bottle or is being patted on the behind, and destroying our eardrums if I'm a second late feeding or changing. He'll be a strong

Breton duke, my lady. Now you have a good time, you and His Majesty. Oh, I nearly forgot. Monsieur Marot asked me to enclose these verses – he said you'd asked his son, Clément, for them.

(At that moment Geneviève is joined by the bard Jean Marot, leading and urging his son. Clément shyly bows and recites the poem Anne asked for. The audience hears only a portion of it.)

Willingly in this very month

The earth moistens and renews.

Many lovers do the same.

My manner of loving is not so,

My loves last for all seasons.

There is no damsel so fair

whose beauty does not waver.

Ugliness draws them into its gondola.

. . .nothing can diminish the fairness of my lady

And thus, since she be forever beautiful,

my love lasts for all time.

The lady for whom

I bear this passion

Is Virtue. She whom

true lovers call the eternal nymph. Good lovers, come, says she.

Come to me, I await you.

Come...

My love lasts for all time.

Prince, have this immortal friend

and apply yourself to love her eternally,

Then may you recompense without ruse.

My love lasts for all time. (17)

(Geneviève claps her hands in appreciation and Jean Marot nods his head and bows. He leads Clément offstage whence they had come. Anne smiles in pleasure and amusement upon hearing the poem. Geneviève picks up a broom and starts sweeping. She looks up suddenly)

GENEVIÈVE

Now rest, my lady. Be as good to yourself as you are to the Lord and to your husband. Your child is sweet and well. There's naught for you to worry about. *(suddenly curtseys low with solemnity)* My respect to His Majesty and his lordship, the King.

(Queen Anne reacts happily, sighing with relief. Geneviève remains standing, puts the towel back on her shoulder, and takes from her apron pocket a letter which she unfolds and begins to read. Its contents are spoken aloud by the Queen who writes while she speaks to the audience, as if the audience were the recipient of the letter)

QUEEN ANNE

My little Orlando – I am so proud to have this cherub. Who nurses him in my absence? Make sure you have a gentlewoman with full abundant breasts which give good milk. I would that I were there to feed him and watch my little prince. I know my place is with him, but the dukes of Brittany have always been stronger than kings and my king's weaknesses express to me a greater need. My little Orlando. Write to me of him, Geneviève. Monsieur Marot and little Clément, you have given to me and to my son reassuring lyrics.

(Lights fade. Then they are relit after a moment of transition. Anne is seated as before, but wears a shawl around her shoulders. The bedroom seems less gay. A great deal of activity to and fro, including a doctor examining the baby. Anne appears to be reading her letter as before. Geneviève, somewhat tired and worried, comes out from the bedroom, in front of the balcony window as before)

GENEVIÈVE

Greetings to you, my lady. You must be enjoying the carnivals and the beautiful cafés of Lyon. Are you well? Indeed, His Majesty has done very well in his invasion. Every Italian seems to love him. *(mood change)* The weather's cold again, my lady. Charles is pretty well but we're watching his cough and occasional sniffles. *(Anne stands up in alarm; Geneviève, predicting her fear, says in reassurance)* Now, now, there is nothing serious, Your Majesty. The doctor is with him. *(Geneviève stops, bewildered by her own anxiety)* We're feeding him special liquids. He can't seem to keep down his food, if you understand; his little stomach doesn't want to co-operate and he cries and cries and cries until I sing to him and rock him to sleep. He's a lovely lad. Now, don't you worry, love, we're giving him good care and he's a fighter. He'll be all right – lord, my lady Anne, I nursed you and your sister through the same childhood maladies.

(Anne seems a little more relieved but still somewhat worried. Geneviève raises her hand in which she silently follows a letter, Anne's response.)

QUEEN ANNE

My Lord in Heaven, Geneviève, what happens to my boy? Leave him not a minute! Allow no one but yourself to touch his food. I await my king's return from Italy. Then we will be off. In six days, we will depart and hurry back to Amboise. Take care of my child, Geneviève.

(*Lights turn off. Then after a minute they are on again. We see lower centre forestage, at a table, a character from the first scene of Act One, Duchesse Louise de Savoie. She is seated at an angle, turned slightly to the left of the stage but seated at her table exactly in the middle of centre forestage. Well behind her, on a well-raised platform so as to be well seen, is Cesare Borgia. He sits at a right angle to the audience facing rightstage, the opposite direction of the angle towards which Savoie faces silently. Borgia is seated comfortably in an ornate chair of Venetian design with a short iron back to it. Behind him can be deciphered the shadows but not the faces of Pope Alexander and Galeazzo Sforza. On left stage is the Lyonnaise chamber of Anne and on right stage is the balcony-windowed room, both from the immediately preceding scenes. Queen Anne is wearing a headpiece with a cloth that covers her hair and neck. Her dress is long-sleeved, simple and very long. The room on rightstage is slightly darkened. It has the curtains drawn through which there is only a still room, with a maid sitting quietly. Queen Anne receives from a messenger, accompanied by a priest, a rolled manuscript which she slowly unfolds. At the same time Borgia also unrolls also a letter on parchment, holding it out in front of him. Below him Lady Louise de Savoie begins to write and speak. Geneviève emerges from the still room on the right and also begins to speak. She has a vacant, disheartened weariness in her walk. The speech of Savoie alternates with that of Geneviève)*

SAVOIE

My lord Cesare Borgia, I bring more vital news to you of the French court at Amboise.

GENEVIÈVE

My lady Anne, I bear you sad tidings of your lad.

SAVOIE

The Valois threat is gone. The heir to the throne of Charles and Anne died moments ago in infancy.

(Cesare smiles, eyes flashing and behind him the shadow of Alexander VI nods in approval)

GENEVIÈVE

Your infant, my sweet lady, passed away into the shadows. His malady was inexplicable. He went from a little cough to fitful tremors and sickness. *(pause)* No child had ever died in my arms.

(Queen Anne turns pale from shock and cries out, gripping her table, eyes wide and flaming; the priest and the messenger in her room come to her and attempt vainly to comfort her. The priest finally waves the messenger away, picks up the letter thrown to the ground and places it on the table. As he wipes the Queen's brow with a cool, moist cloth, he stands supportively beside her, and she finishes reading the letter. Queen Anne looks at the letter to begin reading again only when it is Geneviève's turn to speak again)

SAVOIE

There is no further obstacle. If and when Charles is no more, the political threat to Italy is gone. Duke d'Orléans, in immediate succession to His Majesty, has declared guardianship of my infant son, François. No other child will impede the ascendancy of the dukes of Savoie to the throne of France. The next generation of French kings will renounce its claims to Italy, as I have promised you. My boy, François, will be King of France.

GENEVIÈVE

To comfort you, my Queen, my Duchess, there is no way. God owes you an answer, if not a reckoning. *(pause)* Why? Oh, my sweet, if I could cover your eyes and keep you from feeling pain, I would have long ago. *(pause)* How? There are spies in our court, lady – I can feel the hardness and danger. Go to your husband. Let him comfort you, love. And then, soon, you'll try again. *(a bit of hope in Anne's eyes)*

SAVOIE

François is too close, and Italy must safeguard its power. Louis, Duke d'Orléans, must ascend the throne before my son becomes the recognised heir. Should there be further obstacles, I urge your lordships to act with expediency.

(Cesare Borgia calls a young valet to attend him and to write what he recites. As he speaks, Louise de Savoie reads his letter)

BORGIA

Madame Duchesse de la Savoie et d'Anjou – there will be no further obstacles, Madame. Our enemies no longer menace us. Pietro de Medici and his family are regarded as traitors for his attempted negotiation with France. Ludovico Sforza betrayed Charles to join the Holy League of Pope Alexander and now the Milanese soldiers shall destroy completely the French garrisons in Italy. My father, Pope Alexander, and I have joined in coalition with Venice, England, Spain and the Austrian Empire against King Charles.

France will be driven out of Italy. Nothing of the Franks will remain in our country but the smoke of battle. But the news of the termination of the Valois lineage is well received, Madame. We had. . . 'suspected' that Orlando *might* not survive. It is our determined belief, Lady Savoie, that if Charles should have other male heirs, they would lack the strength to. . . sustain the terrible pestilence and diseases of our time. *(A terrible sense of evil is apparent in Borgia)* Our congratulations to you, Madame, on the eventual succession of François, your son. *(pause)* For the time being, however, we of the Holy League feel that, once Charles is driven out, he will pose no further danger. We sense there may be advantages, should Louis d'Orléans come to the throne. *(pause)* Be patient, for your son, my lady, *will* reign soon enough. And should King Charles and Queen Anne conceive more princes, we will refuse them life. We thank you for your services, Lady Savoie, and *assure* you that there will be no further impediments.

GENEVIÈVE

My lady Anne, take heart. You *will* bring more children, *and an heir*, to life.

END OF SCENE IV

SCENE V

(Two years after the previous scene. Stage showing scene of a ballroom in the Amboise palace of Charles VIII. Couples are mingling – military officers and their ladies, aristocrats and their wives, mistresses, barons, dukes. Charles VIII and his cousin, Duke Louis d'Orléans, stand apart)

CHARLES VIII

Lady Anne remains in perpetual mourning. Thrice she has given birth to an heir. And thrice has the boy died, despite the most protective, exacting care. Mysterious, incomprehensible. It is my punishment, perhaps. Pursuing a doomed policy of conquest in a foreign land.

D'ORLÉANS

Yours was a victorious battle.

CHARLES VIII

Aye, but a battle of retreat. My remaining troops in Italy were vanquished. All territory fell to the Spanish, and the little dictators resumed their power.

D'ORLÉANS

There will be other political victories, Charles. *(pausing)* I owe you my life – again – my cousin. . . and my honour.

(Charles VIII attempts to stop his expression of gratitude with embarrassed gestures). I pray you, I would have you know that I will not forget your decision to refuse a safe, honourable departure, so that you might return with your forces to give assistance to myself and my

troops, trapped by Sforza's armies. Had you not turned back, Charles, you would not have seen us bleed. Had you not turned back, my cousin, you would have left Italy without being chased, with honour; and Sforza, Ludovico Sforza, would have slain us – my men and me.

CHARLES VIII

I trusted too many of them – Alexander, the Medicis and Borgia. But Sforza above all was my ally – how he swore allegiance to me, Louis, how he welcomed me into his land, into Milan! *(putting his hand to his head, disheartened)* How he betrayed me – my ally, my friend – when opportunity arose! *(shaking off his mood, says proudly)* When I return to Milan, he shall be sought out and punished for his duplicity.

D'ORLÉANS

(Looking intensely at Charles) I promise you, Charles, *(slowly)* I shall avenge this betrayal, I shall avenge Italy. *(pause)* I would give my freedom to see the Queen smile and laugh again.

CHARLES VIII

There is no comforting her. She has returned already to the solace of her native Brittany. To her, it is a greater tragedy to have no successor to her dukedom than whether or not France has an heir.

D'ORLÉANS

Aye, *(with melancholy smile)* it has always been so.

CHARLES VIII

(eyeing Louis, half amused, half envious) There is no disputing Louis, that my wife inspires no less passion in you, my cousin, than in myself. *(no response from Louis)* And what of Jeanne, my sister,

whom you married well before the Breton wars, before I ended my sister's regency, before I became king in my own right?

D'ORLÉANS

(stiffening) Your Majesty remembers the conditions of my marriage.

CHARLES VIII

Aye. Though Jeanne be my sister, were I her husband, I would find physical love with her difficult.

D'ORLÉANS

There has been none.

CHARLES VIII

(laughs in disbelief) Oh, come now, friend and cousin. You and I, we both revel in nurturing the most dishonourable, the most lascivious

infidelities in Europe. Women do not pass our grasp. Even the most unbecoming of wives provokes desire within her husband. Even. . . *(Charles says this with sad, painful brotherly guilt)* even the most crippled. . .

D'ORLÉANS

There has been none between us, sir, *(utter seriousness, stiffening. Pause)* but I. . . love the lady's soul. *(looking at Charles embarrassedly, sheepishly)* Though life as her husband has been a kind of hell. I cannot bear the sight of her.

CHARLES VIII

(reflecting, comprehending, yet a bit shocked) It was Jeanne who came to me to plead for your freedom. It was she who awakened me to the brutality of your imprisonment. It was Jeanne who deftly suggested that you be released to serve as my emissary to end the Breton wars, to negotiate a marriage settlement with Lady Anne.

D'ORLÉANS

Aye, so I was told. *(reflective. Sees Duchess Louise de Savoie with courtiers and Cesare Borgia, who enter)* My wife deserves the joys of a passionate lover. *(Looks carefully at couple – Savoie and Borgia – and turns after a brief silence)* You remember, surely, the Duke de Savoie's heroic death two years ago, at the beginning of your expedition to Milan? *(Charles nods. Louis looks distrustfully at the couple Savoie and Borgia near the back of the room)* I gave the Duke's boy, François, my legal guardianship, partly out of friendship for my brave friend and partly out of the need for a healthy child of my own, which marriage will never bring me. *(Charles, moved, touches his cousin's shoulder)* But I am stunned at the quick recovery of the Duchess de Savoie from the pangs of widowhood. *(nodding to the couple)* See there, with her is your former adversary – Borgia – whose family feigned peaceful support and co-operation with Your Majesty. Strange and perhaps dangerous bedfellows. *(looks at them intensely with suspicion)*

CHARLES VIII

Anne cannot abide either. I believe the Duchess is most jealous of the Queen. Diplomacy forces me to tolerate Borgia's presence in my court.

(*Louis begins to comprehend certain things, revealed by his facial expression and a short reflective silence as he watches the couple. Queen Anne enters. Both Charles and Louis join her and offer her an arm. King Charles takes her hand and kisses it*)

CHARLES VIII

A lovely gown, my lady Anne.

D'ORLÉANS

(*smiles at Anne as she turns to him in wistful pleasure and he holds her two hands with his own, against his chest. He looks at her in gentle teasing*) Who be this lovely lass?

QUEEN ANNE

I am Duchess of the Bretons. *(Sad but dignified yet obviously much more introverted)* Some say I am a queen as well, but I prefer to be the Breton duchess: *(looks around and then at Louis and says, playfully, in a whisper)* more power and fewer enemies.

D'ORLÉANS

The Duchess *is* a Queen, I'm afraid. Her court attends her.

(Louis d'Orléans leads her towards Charles to whom Louis gives her hand. Charles brings her to the centre of the floor and begins a slow, dignified medieval dance. (18) After they have danced for a few minutes, other couples follow suit. The music slows and shortly after the royal couple leaves the dance floor)

CHARLES VIII

My Queen, my friends and welcome company, come to the freshly cleaned and polished chamber to watch a new sport, a leisure game of tennis ball.

(Charles leads Anne from the ball to her apartment to retrieve her shawl. To do this they move left downstage. Charles then leads Anne down through a corridor, old and dilapidated. Thus others except for Anne will not see the accident and remain oblivious to it. The roof of corridor is very low, so low that Charles, not withstanding his diminutive stature, strikes his head against the archway. The accident seems slight. By this time, they have arrived lower right stage while his company attends them upper right stage. An arched entrance separates Anne and Charles from the rest of the party. Charles is stunned, holding his hands over his head, standing apart. Queen Anne calls out, "My lord!" and holds his head in her arms. Hearing the Queen, d'Orléans and his guards arrive and help the King up again, who is apparently only dazed. The party of the court stands more upperstage on the other side of the arch, light focusing on the figures of Anne, Charles and Louis. Hushes among the court present. When

the King, accompanied by Anne and Louis, smiling, a bit dazed, bids his company enter, relief and dignified gaiety is resumed. Lights fade slowly. Then trumpets are heard. The arched passageway is removed, and the King and Queen take their seats. As lights come up again, an imaginary tournament begins. Charles and Anne appear to be watching a game of tennis ball offstage. Charles faces right offstage. His company is behind him. The players' moving shadow are seen against backstage beside him. Anne sits beside him, at an angle, so that both may be seen. Louis stands lower stage, watching the game with interest. There is periodic support and cheering from the company and the royal king and queen. In the course of the third or fourth set the King is smiling, joking, when suddenly he puts his hand to his head and makes a gesture to indicate that he is dazed and in pain. He stands, tries to move but falls forward on his knees, clasping his sword. Queen Anne moves to him and caresses his head)

CHARLES VIII

When I rode into Naples, I entered on a chariot drawn by four white horses, holding in one hand a golden orb and in the other the rod of empire. *(suddenly frightened, feeling the approach of darkness)*

'O celestial father! Grant a place

among the chosen to your loyal

martyr. . .' (19)

(Charles falls into a stupor, disoriented and lost in an imaginative quest; he unsheathes his sword, stares at it and clasps it to him)

'O Durendal! how wouldst thou

become so cruel to Roland,

your master! . . .' (20)

(dies)

QUEEN ANNE

(Pause, holds her husband's head against her until she feels the breath leave his body. Then she lays him back gently. She wipes the

perspiration from his brow and moves her hand tenderly through his hair, as if she were still protecting him from the pain of his dreams)

'The soul of the audacious pagan, who for so long has borne himself so arrogant and so proud, emerges from his body colder than ice, and flees in blasphemy towards the ghastly shores of the Acheron. . .' (21)

(pause. Then she rises and announces quietly to the party) The King is dead!

END OF SCENE V

A few minutes before beginning of Act Five, musicians will perform 'Le mariage insolite de Marie la Bretonne' (22). As the curtains rise, the song will be ending.

ACT FIVE

SCENE I

(Outside Nantes, a small hamlet and large field. Workers in medieval peasant costume. Peasants suddenly kneel and incline the head. A convoy approaches with Duchess Anne, Philippe de Montauban, Geneviève and a couple of guards and a valet. Duchess Anne dismounts. The others follow suit, but, only Philippe and Geneviève walk behind the Duchess, unobtrusively)

DUCHESS ANNE

(Speaks to peasants) Carry on, please.

(Duchess Anne walks quickly at a determined pace to left upperstage and climbs on to a small hill. Philippe follows. She reaches a wide brook that crosses her path and prepares to remove her shoes to cross it. A peasant, alarmed, tries to come to her rescue)

PEASANT

If the Duchess would permit. . . *(by his gesture, offers to lift her over. She refuses)*

DUCHESS ANNE

Nay, good fellow, I have waited years to feel the Loire waters of Nantes again. Save your strength for my lady-in-waiting.

(Geneviève is she to whom the Duchess gestures nonchalantly. Duchess Anne walks with pleasure and relief through the stream. Geneviève, having put on a stocky coquettish appearance, comes hurrying up, exhausted and breathless from chasing after Duchess Anne)

PEASANT

(Obediently picks up Geneviève and says to her) Permit me, lady.

(Geneviève, surprised and shocked at what appears to be at first manhandling, realises the courtesy. Flattered, her sensually aroused manner is comical. She continues to keep her arms around the peasant's neck after he puts her down. And, embarrassed, finally releases him. The peasant, very tall but muscular, stares at Geneviève voluptuously. Geneviève is comically flirtatious with him. Duchess Anne and Philippe look back at them, amused, with muffled laughter. Philippe smiles, takes Duchess Anne's arm and helps her over a steep rock as they circle back centre stage. The peasants have moved further to the left, away from the central action)

PHILIPPE DE MONTAUBAN

I see the Duchess has finally shed her widow's weeds. No doubt 'tis good to feel Breton soil again. *(looking around, breathing happily and well)*

DUCHESS ANNE

Aye. *(sighs and give a breath of relief)* The air is cleaner here, near the sea. I can breathe nowhere else. Our soil is not the best for cultivation of cereal or fruit, but the lamb and oxen graze here in plenty, in peace.

(Watches the peasants work the land for a few moments, walks over to them, staring at the earth, puzzled) This persistent chalked clay of our earth. Some day it may prove a valuable mineral to times more advanced than our own. *(bends down and, taking a handful of soil, lets it sift through her hand)* But for now, we must find a way to nourish the land. *(reflectively)* Philippe, have several tons of dung and cow excrement transported immediately from the northern pastures of Brittany. There *are* other substances we may use to fertilise this barren, chalky earth. I have been reading of a new science of the land, Philippe. We must learn more from this area of learning called agronomy.

PHILIPPE

(surprised, inclines in pleasure) Yes, my lady.

(pause, change of tone) The ship of which I spoke is moored over there, Lady Anne.

(He points to the wreckage of a merchant ship which, before in shadows, now becomes visible through lighting.

Meanwhile Geneviève and the peasant frolic comically; he is pursuing, she is running and laughing. Geneviève finally runs into a barn downstage left; the peasant follows. He takes off his boots and hat and goes in after her; wicked sexual laughter is heard. Anne looks amused but disapproving)

DUCHESS ANNE

(justifying her abstention of reproval and judgement, uncomfortable, yet amused) She raised me, you see. She cared for all of my children and saw more of their tears than ever I would know. *(pause)* I have no right to dictate morality to her. Let her frolic. We are all joyful to be returning to our land. *(pause, then in a*

serious, businesslike tone) So! We have further problems of piracy. How many of our ships have thus been attacked this last year alone? One hundred, did you say?

PHILIPPE

One hundred and ten, to be precise, over the last three years. Oftimes they are travellers, priests, traders with their families, or simply a merchant crew. Generally, there are no survivors, such as this one taken. *(Gestures to the ship before them)* This is a case of particularly cruel violence: the travellers obviously attempted resistance and were mercilessly executed. Occasionally, lives are spared; only the goods are seized, the sailors and officers set adrift.

DUCHESS ANNE

And the measures approved and begun to police the Loire waters were not continued after my departure. *(bitterly)* Would that Charles had not taken from me the right to rule the land I know best! The authority and order of the Breton dukedom ravaged. Parliament eliminated and replaced by French government. Yea, a tax here and there reduced or eliminated, but no will to improve the life or land of Brittany. Only a puppet bureaucracy answerable in pure fact to Charles: the end of autonomy.

(pause, return to subject of piracy, looking with disbelief at the remains of the ship) Who does this, Philippe? Is it an act of aggression or simple brutal robbery?

PHILIPPE

A bit of both, Duchess. But never attributable to a particular government policy or precise order. In view of your absence from Brittany, Spain, England and Portugal have closed their eyes to the plundering of our merchant and naval vessels.

DUCHESS ANNE

And the Governor of Brittany, Louis de la Trémouille, whom I had appointed to administer in my place, who became my husband's marionette, has done nothing: no enforcement of our laws, of the protective rulings passed before my departure?

PHILIPPE

Nay. Most effective in combat, the governor was but indifferent to the welfare of the Bretons – an incompetent administrator. For three years he lived off our land and taxes. But now your Ladyship has returned. *(This last line is said with pleasure and relief. Pause)* The pirates come from foreign shores, but our neighbours make no effort to safeguard their waters and their vermin float freely to ravish the Bretons.

DUCHESS ANNE

Well, this useless figurehead of Charles has been dismissed by my order. Henceforth we will police the coasts and outlying waterways thoroughly. I will reassemble Parliament and request the re-enactment of former protective laws and naval appropriations. I will request that Parliament sanction immediately the rights and means to pursue and punish the pirates of the channel and coastal waters. *(pause, then said with weariness again)* How I am sick to see the unkind indifference of our so-called friends! Look, *(pointing)* a silk scarf and a doll! What immeasurable greed! *(stands up and moves downstage left)* I have been gone too long, Philippe. *(begins to walk purposefully towards right downstage)* When I returned to visit my homeland after the death of my eldest, the Bretons were most gracious. . . but distant. I had become Queen of France, and they regarded me as a stranger to their land. Your magistrates would bow to me and applaud my restoration of the ducal palace and the increased capacities I directed of my father's château. These were harmless matters, they thought, which did not interfere with the power of true government. But my King and Brittany's governor and ruling class no longer expected my presence in the Breton Parliament. In fact, they could not abide it. The deputies among the magistrates and the nobility were resentful of my power as they had always been. The people seem to remember, to have some distant memory of the duchess of the wooden shoes, and they welcome me back without truly knowing or remembering anything more of me than legend. But that is enough for them and for me. I could not ask that they remember the laws we promulgated to keep the noblemen's hunters and mercenary plunderers off their pastures and fields, or the decrease in taxes, or the prosperous trade we brought to this land before the wars with France, the cathedrals and chapels we built, the towns we rendered free by charter. Nor could I ask that they remember all that they lost to the plague, all that they have given in labour, money and blood to the wars. I can only ask that they remember me as the embodiment of that which once was and to think of what still may be – sovereignty. Yea, the people of Brittany seem to recall who I am. Thank God. But Brittany's magistrates and nobility... they are forever hostile, as they have always been. *(pause, then with melancholy)* Before I left to marry, you and I, Philippe, had built the strongest marine force Brittany or France had ever known. Since my departure the best of our forces, the most well-equipped and finest of our ships, have served the King of France against the English attacks in Normandy; and Brittany is left with the shambles of its past naval excellence, diminished by war and piracy. *(pause, and then quietly and steadily)* We will restore our ships and fleets, and never again will the harbours of Brest and the eastern ports of Morbihan be visited by invasion or destruction. *(pause, then quietly, with self-reproach)* I sacrificed too much by marrying. I am back now.

PHILIPPE

But Lady Anne... You are bound, by contract, to marry Charles's successor, that is, our old friend the Duke d'Orléans.

DUCHESS ANNE

Who will be crowned shortly as Louis XII. True, I am bound by human law to marry a man and a king; although I do love the man, I hate the king. Nature bids me, in the midst of widowhood, to return to my natural state, that being my role as Duchess of Brittany, the role I have resumed. As Duchess of Brittany, I am bound to hate the King of France. But as a woman, I deny not that I care most deeply for the man, Duke Louis d'Orléans. Yet even though I am bound by human law to marry Louis d'Orléans, King of France, it is divine law which forbids Louis's divorce. *(pause, then firmly, simply)* He has a wife, a marriage sanctioned and blessed by the Church, by God. Louis has many talents, Philippe, but divorce without sin or excommunication is beyond possibility. In any case, if I marry again, the price will not be as high. Brittany will remain sovereign, I promise you. *(pause, then change of mood and tone, more relaxed and cheerful)* Come, let us depart – it is late and your young wife expects you with your supper.

(calls to Geneviève as Philippe readies himself to resume riding) Geneviève! Geneviève!

GENEVIÈVE

Coming, lady! *(calling out from inside the barn)* Yves was showing me... about...

(Philippe and Duchess Anne glance at each other in amusement and, laughing, exit offstage right after rejoining their convoy. After a few moments, Geneviève comes out of the barn, making a few gestures to tidy up her hair and costume. We hear again Duchess Anne call, "Geneviève!" Geneviève again calls offstage to Duchess Anne, "Coming, my lady." Geneviève begins to readjust her headdress and cape in a hurried manner. Her companion comes out of the barn now

and we see him in a far more disoriented, dazed and tousled state than Geneviève. The fact is that he walks with difficulty, comically. He falls to the ground, landing on his knees by a bucket of water and pours the bucket of water on himself. He exhibits relief, saying, "Ah, c'est bon!" two or three times, and wanders over to his boots and hat. As he struggles to put his boots back on, Geneviève prepares to return to her mistress's convoy. Duchess Anne continues to call her from offstage and Geneviève continues to respond)

GENEVIÈVE

Oh, what a delightful fellow! No matching good Breton stock. *(She is speaking to the audience laughing and smiling mischievously)* Oh, it's been years since I –

(She breaks off, reddens, having suddenly realised the impropriety. Embarrassed, she clears her throat and attempts a serious demeanour, looking back flirtatiously now and then at the peasant. She continues to tidy herself. Suddenly a priest appears upper stage right and with him is a litter carried by French royal guards. In the litter is a more mature man in the ecclesiastical dress of an archbishop. We will see

that it is the Archbishop Georges Amboise, close friend and counsellor to the King's successor – Louis d'Orléans. The Archbishop descends, and the priest approaches Geneviève. Geneviève continues to tidy herself)

PRIEST

Good lady, my lord Archbishop Amboise of Rouen, counsellor to the King of France, begs an audience with your mistress, Lady Anne.

(Geneviève turns to the audience and, with a gesture of the hand, cuts off the speech of the priest and stops the action. All movement on stage except for that of Geneviève freezes)

GENEVIÈVE

We'll need to stop here now. There's more to be explained.

(The scene, except for Geneviève, falls into shadow)

END OF SCENE I

SCENE II

GENEVIÈVE

(Completing her tidying-up) Well, as you may understand, the Duchess, my Lady Anne, is holding out most determinedly against the politicians. But in the end, as we all know, she will have to marry Louis. Not that she had not yearned to do so since the day they met. But, it's like all those histories that speak of duty and love as opposing priorities which inhibit true decision and action. Well, this being a drama, a play based on action that must be shown, we can't dwell too long on emotional indecision. So we'll have to speed things up a bit and unravel the main bits of the story.

(Lights come up downstage left on Pope Alexander VI) Here is old Alex VI, the Pope. He's heard the news of King Charles's death and is making plans for alliance with Louis XII, the new French king. Old Alex has married his daughter Lucrezia to the Prince of Salerno, a natural son of the late King Alphonso II of Naples. Alexander had also been trying to arrange a marriage between his son Cesare and the

daughter of the present king of Castile, Federico, also King of Naples. But Federico got suspicious, as any natural living creature would, of the Holy Pontiff and his greedy demands. Alexander – the Pope I'm speaking of – demanded that the entire principality of Taranto be given as the dowry. Now, that would have just been too compromising for Federico so he refused. Well, Alexander and Borgia were angry and, to avenge themselves and provoke political problems for Federico, they decided to seek an alliance with France, with Louis d'Orléans. By coincidence, the daughter of Federico promised to Cesare Borgia was Princess Charlotte of Naples who had been brought up in the French court and was still residing there under royal protection.

(lights come up an another scene) There's Louis. He's just begun his reign. Next to him, standing, is Georges Amboise, Archbishop of Rouen, the closest friend and adviser to Louis in these latter years. One of the first of Louis's official actions upon becoming king was to dispatch letters to all the princes of Italy, proclaiming his immediate intention to recover France's Italian possessions, his by right through his grandmother, Valentina Visconti of Milan. Pope Alexander and

his son Cesare were pleased as could be, as this was their chance to recover power and vengeance against all the other Italian princes and against Federico of Castile. The Pope immediately sent congratulations to Louis upon his accession to the throne of France.

(We see the lights on Pope Alexander left downstage fade and Geneviève walks left also. The scene and lighting focuses on Louis XII, Duke d'Orléans and King of France, lower right downstage.

He is dictating aloud to his secretary. Smiling and sauntering back and forth across the room. Louis, in this scene, has aged a bit more but is still physically stronger and younger than in Scene I of Act One. He is perhaps at the peak of his strength and manly attractiveness, a mature and virile man of forty. Georges Amboise stands but, in the course of the dictation, from time to time sits and reads 'The Discourses' of Machiavelli. Louis dictates)

LOUIS XII

We thank your Holy Eminence for the prompt attention. It is with eager pleasure we assure you that I will not lose sight of the Vatican's interests nor will I fail to advance those of Borgia's name. I will most certainly pursue and arrange the union your Holy Eminence seeks between your godson Cesare Valentine Borgia and Princess Charlotte, and I bear to you the wish that you grant me the pleasure of according the lands of Dauphinois to great Cesare's possession.

(Georges Amboise smiles, amused by the generous, teasing tone and exchanges knowing glances with Louis. Then Amboise returns to sit and begins to read). What do you study so, Georges? Theophrastes's 'Consolation of Philosophy'? Ovid's 'Histories'?

AMBOISE

Nay, my lord. A young secretary of Florence, attached to Savonarola's crumbling government, has written tracts on the art of politics. Most instructive. Niccoló di Machiavelli, he is called.

Perhaps he will write of you, Your Majesty, when you reconquer Italy.

LOUIS XII

(laughs) Perhaps. We shall see. He has written of Charles, at times pejoratively. *(He continues his dictation and Amboise continues to read)* I propose to your Holy Eminence, Pope Alexander VI, that the following be granted to Cesare Borgia: the hand of Princess Charlotte of Naples, the lands of the Dauphinois and an annual pension of 20,000 livres; Borgia shall be proclaimed as well Captain of a Hundred Lances, one of France's most coveted prestigious honours.

(Louis and Amboise exchange a laugh. Obviously, this last honour was invented by Louis) All of this will be granted upon four conditions: Firstly, I must obtain from your Holy Eminence an annulment of my marriage to Princess Jeanne de France and accordingly, full permission to form a union with Duchess Anne of Brittany; secondly, that the Vatican support and assist my rightful claim to the Visconti family possession of Milan; thirdly, that

Ludovico Sforza be delivered to my forces to be punished for his treachery against the former King of France – Charles VIII, my cousin; fourthly, that your Holy Eminence recognises the exceptional merit of my faithful friend and counsellor, Archbishop Georges Amboise and thereby grant to him the rank of cardinal.

(Amboise looks up, surprised, and meets humbly the intensely penetrating gaze of Louis XII. Lights fade)

END OF SCENE II

SCENE III

(Lights come up on Geneviève, lower leftstage)

GENEVIÈVE

Well, the Pope couldn't say no. And plans were made immediately for Cesare to march gloriously into Chinon, the King's castle. Louis had sent a special ambassador to Rome to bring the son of the Pope to France.

(Following action is pantomimed lower and upper right stage to illustrate events described by Geneviève.)

As soon as Borgia gave up the cardinal cap, King Louis conferred upon him the title of Duke de Valentinois and Captain of a Hundred Lances, with a most generous yearly revenue. And, of course, the promised marriage with Princess Charlotte of Naples was arranged, much to the poor lady's panic and chagrin. Oh, the costumes, music, expense Louis went to, just to feed and satisfy Borgia's extravagant vanity! A month of festivity, dancing, splendour. Finally, when the time came to meet Louis's condition for the annulment of his marriage to Jeanne, well . . .

(As Geneviève finishes these lines, she moves slowly to the right and lights come up on centre and downstage left. Downstage left, Borgia is seated comfortably, drinking and eating. He is enjoying the company of ladies and a singer with guitar. To the right are King Louis and Amboise in a separate room, with the nuncio at Paris. Their room is quiet, with dimmed light. To the left a curtain half-closed separates the rooms. The King stands beside the curtain,

looking with amused curiosity at Borgia and his entertainment. Amboise stands on the opposite right facing the King. The nuncio is sitting meditatively on the bench placed against the back wall. A window is above him)

LOUIS XII

There he sits wallowing in my court; well beyond a month he has tried my patience. Repeat this again to me, Georges.

GEORGES AMBOISE

The Duke de Valentinois Cesare Valentine Borgia regrets that he has not in his possession the promised dispensation to allow you to marry Duchess Anne. He assures Your Majesty, however, that Pope Alexander will send it soon.

LOUIS XII

(pause, smiles and with a glint in his eye) How dare he sully my court with no intention of keeping his word! Does he think me so

lame-minded to believe that he would set foot in France without this document? Nay, though no less cruel, his father knows the limits of a lie better than Borgia. I have written acceptance of my conditions from the Pope. His letters assure me that Borgia carries with him all that I asked.

AMBOISE

Even greater proof exists, my lord.

LOUIS XII

Eh?

AMBOISE

There sits in respectful prayer *(gesturing and pointing to the Bishop-Nuncio)* the Bishop of Setta, Nuncio of Paris, the Vatican's religious representative in France. I persuaded him to come to the court.

(calls to the Bishop-Nuncio) My friend, Monsieur Arrezzo.

(He approaches, bowing fearfully)

LOUIS XII

You know something of this matter, Monseigneur?

ARREZZO

Your Majesty. *(bowing)*

LOUIS XII

Speak, sir, of my dispensation!

ARREZZO

(Surprised and disturbed) Why? Are you dissatisfied, my lord? It was confided to our delegation that Signor Borgia and his Holy Eminence had prepared carefully all official documents. Your Majesty must be most pleased with the draughtsmanship. Upon the

arrival in Chinon of Lord Borgia, I myself was asked to add my signature in apposition, next to that of his Holy Worship Pope Alexander VI. *(sudden comprehensive look from Louis)* I assure Your Majesty that the documents we offer you are valid and complete. My secretary and I scrutinised them word by word our first evening in Chinon while Lord Borgia and Your Majesty were in discussion.

LOUIS XII

Indeed. *(Smiling at Georges Amboise, who returns his knowing gaze)* Thank you, Monseigneur. I am most particularly satisfied with your earnest workmanship.

(The Nuncio, flattered, bows and exits, goes into the next room and bows to Borgia. Borgia looks up, sees the Nuncio and behind him King Louis XII. Borgia comprehends the exposure of his ruse. He continues to drink coolly, his eyes hateful and calculating. But he assumes a friendly duplicitous smile in acknowledging the Nuncio, Bishop Arrezzo. Louis follows Arrezzo into the room and, as he does

so, everyone but Borgia bows low. Borgia inclines his head with token courtesy.

Good company and good wine. *(picks up the bottle on the table)* I am told you have many vineyards, Cesare, and that your bastards crush the grapes between their thighs until the juice of the fruit is indistinguishable from human blood. Is that true?

BORGIA

(smiling) That is a French custom. My vineyards bear white grapes.

LOUIS XII

Ah. *(sits beside Cesare and drinks)* I have found, Cesare, a solution to this dispensation we await: that you assure me the Pope is sending the document, although His Eminence in his letters to me promised it would be in your possession when you arrived and the Nuncio of Paris has confirmed seeing it, signing it and reading it the evening of your arrival. *(Louis pauses cunningly. Silent uncomfortable reaction from Borgia)* Whatever the case may be, if the Pope will be sending the dispensation later, as you say, then he *has* given *his consent*. I, therefore, am convoking an assembly of theologians in order that they decide to pronounce the legal dissolution of my marriage immediately. After all, your father – forgive me *(sarcastic or merely ironic)* – His Holy Eminence the Pope *is* sending the letter: that is, he *has* dispatched his consent. Knowing this, the rest is a legal formality. I will inform you of the council's decision. Meantime, if you should by chance discover this mysteriously displaced document among your papers, Cesare, *(again irony in his voice)* you will share it with me, won't you?

BORGIA

Most certainly, Your Majesty. I would, with joy, spare you the bother of a theological inquiry. *(smiling. Each understands and gazes with intent at the other)* I will again examine my papers.

LOUIS XII

Excellent! Excellent! Come lady, *(taking the hand of a beautiful woman)* converse with his lordship, for soon he will marry and will drink only with the most powerful Spaniards in Italy.

(laughter, Louis exits. Lights fade.
As lights come up again, we see, also leftstage, a chair and table where Arrezzo studies. He reaches for his cup of wine and drinks it. While he does so, Geneviève speaks)

GENEVIÈVE

Poor Nuncio Arrezzo. Within hours of his innocent visit to Chinon, Borgia has him poisoned.

(Nuncio clutches at the air and falls on the table. Lights on left stage fade)

END OF SCENE III

SCENE IV

(Lights come up again on Geneviève. Left forestage, we see the scene suspended by Geneviève before)

GENEVIÈVE

(Calling out, as if to technicians) No, not yet. There's more to tell.

(Lights on suspended scene are quickly faded as actors walk off, slightly disgruntled. Lights remain on Geneviève)

Well, the King's theological assembly *did* meet and agreed, under strong advisement from King Louis, mind you, to recognise and proclaim the dissolution of his marriage, but only after receiving the testimony of Lady Jeanne. *(shaking her head)* Poor soul! What's more, the King knew that Duchess Anne respected Lady Jeanne and wouldn't even consider marriage to Louis without her consent, let alone that of the Church.

(Lights dim on Geneviève and focus on Lady Jeanne's hunchbacked, deformed figure, centre stage, in a hooded robe. The actress playing this role must convey tenderness, passion and deep sensitivity)

LADY JEANNE

Good Louis, king at last. And so strong and beautiful! *(face reflects the irony of perceiving beauty when she bears none, yet also delight at Louis's elevation)*

My lords, *(pause)* the King bids you dissolve our marriage. Would that the King's will were God's but it is not and therefore, when the King bids this be done, I must say aye in shame: my soul curls up and hides because of my obedience to a man and my disobedience to God. You ask me, my lords, if we were man and wife fully and truly, under God. In so far as our union was sanctioned by God, yes. I am bound to my lord totally. My sensibilities are merged with his. I delight when he is glad. I rage when he is victimised. I pale when he suffers. If I had been born with the beauty of Diana, I could have given my husband no greater passion. If I had not been born with a monstrous visage, the blush of my desire might have pleased my husband and my beauty might have made him love me. For my soul did not. *(pause)* Aye, our marriage was consummated – in my dreams, in the vacuous flow of my virginal tears. *(pause)* But my lord King Louis, my husband, your hope is to free yourself of our union. Then be it so, if it is your will. I would see you unhappy no longer. I only *fear* for you.

(Lights go out on Jeanne. Stage remains in darkness for a minute or two. We see, as the lights come up, the scene frozen by Geneviève before. Now the actors are in their former positions, motionless: the peasant frozen in a motion of putting on his boots; the priest, mouth open, in the midst of presenting Georges Amboise to Geneviève; Amboise is descending from his litter, motionless as well. Geneviève comes scurrying on from right downstage. She is hurriedly adjusting her cape and headdress again, puffing and out of breath and glancing affectionately and flirtatiously at the peasant as before)

GENEVIÈVE

Right, well, now you understand where we are and all that's going on. We'll take it up where we left *(She snaps her fingers and everyone resumes their actions and role instantly)*

PRIEST

Good lady, my lord Archbishop Amboise, counsellor of the King, begs an audience with your mistress, Lady Anne.

GENEVIÈVE

Aye, Father. The Duchess awaits me further off. Would you follow me, sir?

AMBOISE

(descending with difficulty, because of his great weight) The King follows, good woman, with the intention of a serious discussion and a will to compromise.

(Enter convoy with Anne and Philippe)

DUCHESS ANNE

Geneviève, I bid you, *come* finally.

(As she enters, the party bows. Only when Geneviève gestures does she take notice of them.) Ah, Archbishop, welcome. We were about to return to Nantes!

AMBOISE

A happy coincidence, to meet you on the road to your ladyship's castle.

(A trumpet call is heard, followed by the arrival of King Louis on horseback with three royal guards and a squire)

PRIEST

His Majesty, the King of France.

(Louis dismounts, his squire takes his horse offstage. Louis's guards remain in the background, at attention. Duchess Anne inclines the head but does not bow, as her father, the previous Duke of Brittany, had also refused to do before the King of France. The others bow. King Louis acknowledges all and inclines the head to the Lady Anne, as he had always in the past. He takes her hand and kisses it and replaces it to its position. Then he relaxes a bit, takes off one glove and looks around him with courtesy and interest)

DUCHESS ANNE

You seem most fit, my lord.

LOUIS XII

Aye. . . *(excited, happy)* How fare you, Brett, now that you are home again?

DUCHESS ANNE

Well occupied and in good health, Louis; the séa cleanses grief *(pause)*. There, along the Loire, *(pointing)* with my old faithful Bretons, we have built a canal. The fishermen have re-adapted and found great prosperity in the manmade currents. The peasants are still hungry but less so despite the recalcitrance of our chalky soil. The merchants are no less prosperous but uncomfortable with my change in coinage and further devaluation. But my *nobility*, sir, is *livid* with rage. They had hoped that I'd not come back to Brittany. And they cannot *abide* my courts of poets and illuminators.

LOUIS XII

Hmmph, yes, beware of little barons, Brett – they ambitiously await your second marital absence. We shall have to protect your Breton province more carefully this second time.

DUCHESS ANNE

(pretending not to take notice of the King's implication) See them labouring the ground with Nantes's castle overlooking. *(gazes, above at the sky around them, and studies the scene of the working peasants)* 'Tis the scene of January reproduced here. I am, as you know, the patron of several artists. One named Bourdichon prepared illuminations of the year, scenes from Breton life for each month. It has been graciously prepared for me and is called the 'Livre d'Heures d'Anne de Bretagne'. ('The Book of Hours of Anne of Brittany')

LOUIS XII

Aye, a most beautiful likeness of the court and country.

ANNE

Aye, 'tis blissful, *(pause)* though idealised.

LOUIS XII

Should this be preserved through the centuries, one will know what was the visage and age of Anne de Bretagne.

ANNE

(pause, returning to original topic of conversation) Is there to be a second time?

LOUIS XII

(comprehending, pause) Aye, my lady, there will. Archbishop Amboise accompanies me to assist us in a settlement.

ANNE

How fares Lady Jeanne?

LOUIS XII

To answer you properly, Anne, she suffers quietly and fears for my eternal soul. But... she is no longer my wife.

ANNE

How so? The Pope would not—

LOUIS XII

(cutting her off) This one did. *(calls to Amboise)* Show the dispensation allowing a second marriage for me to the Duchess, Georges.

GEORGES

(Amboise draws up a rolled manuscript and gives it to Duchess Anne.) Here, my lady. And *(drawing out another manuscript)* the decision of our theologians' assembly to dissolve the marriage. And

there, *(pointing to the manuscript)* you see Lady Jeanne's testimony and signature.

ANNE

Aye. *(impressed, studying the manuscript; circumspect yet obviously in command and dignified)*

LOUIS XII

(earnestly with controlled intensity) I wish to us to be married. It has been too long a wait. *(begins to walk with Anne, holding her hand, tenderly)*

ANNE

(walking with him) There are conditions, my lord. I will not be conquered and constrained again, nor will Brittany. Our feelings but not our politics coincide.

LOUIS XII

(letting drop her hand, turning half away; looks around, pauses) It is the end of summer, my lady. I approach the autumn of my life and you remain in my eyes a wounded tender child, rising and falling as the sunlight. And each time releasing an aura of beautiful strength and colour. *(pause)* I have lived, battled beside and contemplated the source of your sunlight, my lady. I, all of men, of all kings, would not obstruct its span or power. I ask only to be your husband. Not as a king but as a man, I embolden myself to remind you of our unspoken sentiments and passion. I bear you great love, my lady.

ANNE

(Looks in same direction where Louis has turned) Would that the years had not separated us; would that I could remove the wounds and unhappy solitude. But now there is light and room for passion, as you say. *(recites from memory Ovid's verse)*

'I no longer fear the shadows which

stealth in the night, nor arms borne for my ruin,

That which I fear is to find you without feeling...

It is you who bear the lightning with which

you may crush me...' (23)

That was a fine verse heard upon the first night you spent in my father's court. *(pause)* My heart and soul are such that I would be the companion of no other man. *(short pause)* But you are now firstly King of France. I am, before all, Brittany's duchess.

LOUIS XII

(Suddenly businesslike) Your conditions, my lady?

ANNE

(becomes harder in manner as well) Firstly... Your promise to return to Brittany the Armorican cities and fortresses taken by Charles and still occupied by royal forces.

LOUIS XII

Done.

ANNE

They will be restored within the year?

AMBOISE

Well before, with the exception of Fougères, which is too badly needed to relinquish, I am afraid.

LOUIS XII

And Nantes of course, where, if you would desire so, my lady, we should be residing a great deal.

ANNE

(back to others) I would desire so.

LOUIS XII

I wish to renew my ties with your land, and the ducal court of Brittany has always been a gay and stimulating haven. *(seeing Anne's emotion)* I would that Brittany's duchess not be uprooted a second time; that, as Queen, she feel no measure of alienation from the quiet courts of Morbihan.

ANNE

That Parliament be re-established at Rennes, with no interference from the king.

LOUIS XII

Acceptable; Charles had dismantled your Parliament, hadn't he, and placed himself at the head of an assembly of states, as in Paris? *(pause)* You have my word, Anne: I shall not interfere.

ANNE

I shall rule as duchess, as before conquest. *(growing in intensity, leaning towards Louis, intimately)* But I will most of all have Brittany strong, independent, not a weak appendage of France. Brittany shall rebuild its marine and naval power, we will reform our judicial courts and police the waters around us so that no more merchants or sailors need be the prey of foreign pirates. We will develop our land and our trade, establish academies of learning and suppress rebellion, without France's supervision.

LOUIS XII

You shall, I know that, Anne.

GEORGES

I do suggest, my lady, that foreign trade agreements pass His Majesty's counsel, before they are signed.

ANNE

I would have economic freedom as well.

LOUIS XII

(waving his hand impatiently at Georges) That is minor, Georges – it is more critical that Lady Anne bears political loyalty to France as well as Brittany. Indeed, that is one point on which I must not compromise. That must be understood between us.

ANNE

(looking steadily at him) It is, my lord. Do we agree on the other matters?

LOUIS XII

(pausing) We do. *(He bows and takes her hand; she inclines her head in emotion)*

ANNE

Then let us marry and seize the joy we were to have had long ago, having satisfied the state and God.

(Lights fade around them until they are seen in profile. Music is heard around them in celebration (24). They turn to the Archbishop, who appears to be joining them in silence. Meanwhile a troubadour sings a love song. Louis and Anne dance a short, romantic celebratory waltz, then embrace and walk out through the passage together. Scene ends. Lights fade. As the scenery is changed behind the curtains, the troubadour continues to play softly)

END OF SCENE IV

SCENE V

(Downstage left Geneviève sits rocking a baby, smiling and delighting in his noises. Downstage right we see Anne and Louis. Louis is very ill in bed and is drowsy, feverish and weak. His bed is parallel to the stage so that the length of his bed is viewed by the audience who faces his side and profile. Anne is seated beside him and faces the audience. Louis is between Anne and the audience)

GENEVIÈVE

(Calling to the other room) Isn't she beautiful, my lady? Your lovely baby girl. . . What will you name her?

LOUIS XII

(weakly yet enthusiastic. . . in response) She will be *Claude*. I would see her, Geneviève.

ANNE

Lie back, my love. The fever's gone, thank heavens, but your bout of sickness was too grave to chance again. I shall not lose a second husband despite the epidemic. . . *(Wipes his brow with a damp cloth. He lies back, exhausted. Anne sees Geneviève approach obediently with Claude)* And I shall not lose another child.

(She takes the baby and holds her in her arms as only a mother can, comes near enough away to keep the baby safe from germs) She is our treasure, Louis.

LOUIS XII

Aye, Brett. That she be. But now, Anne, rest, ye. You have left my side only to give birth. It is I who should be attending you. Geneviève, see that your lady rests. See that. . . See that your lady is well . . . *(tired, falls back on to the pillow)*

(Anne gives the child to Geneviève and goes hurriedly to Louis, pulls the cover over him, begins to feed him gruel)

GENEVIÈVE

He is right, my lady. Come, lie you down in the next chamber with your babe – I'll tend to the King.

(She leads Anne and Claude to the divan in the room. Removes her headdress and covers her with a shawl and blanket. Then returns to find Louis)

'Tis a lovely name, Claude. But what inspires your decision, my lady? *(no answer)* My Lady?. . .

(She glances left stage into the other room and sees that Anne is asleep, her child in her arms, cooing. Geneviève smiles and resumes giving Louis his gruel)

LOUIS XII

We are beholden to Sainte Claude whose shrine the Queen visited in Franche-Comté when she accompanied me to Lyons.

GENEVIÈVE

(feeding Louis) It was a most triumphant return to France, was it not, Your Majesty, after a year in Nantes? And you and my lady were expecting your first child when you left for Milan.

LOUIS XII

I was in Milan when the epidemic struck Blois; Queen Anne fled contagion to Romarantin. *(pausing to eat what Geneviève gives him in several spoonfuls)* But, as you know, the child did not live. I came from Italy to attend her. We conceived another, the survivor in

Anne's arms. The Queen and I believe that Anne's devotion to Sainte Claude is the reason our daughter lives to inherit a kingdom or two; such a tumultuous birth, October last, as we stormed into Milan. Sainte Claude has given us a child and a victory.

(Sounds are heard from the next room. Anne has stretched out, smiling and caressing sleepily the little girl in her arms whom she nurses)

GENEVIÈVE

(As she and Louis look at Anne) Aye, 'tis so well indeed to see her with a life in her arms. Come, now, sir, eat your gruel.

(Louis groans but submits and eats the spoonful offered. A messenger enters quietly and, seeing the Queen asleep, hesitates then coughs. Geneviève hears him and goes to the entrance to speak to him in whispering tones so as to not wake Queen Anne)

MESSENGER

Pardon, lady, Lord Montauban has asked to speak with Duchess Anne on urgent business and Monseigneur Cardinal Amboise has come to announce military victory to his Majesty King Louis.

GENEVIÈVE

(whispering loudly) Do you not see, boy? The Duchess, the Queen, rests and His Majesty lies ill. Go your way, let them be. Neither cardinals nor barons have the privilege of intruding upon the privacy of a young couple, royal, peasant or bourgeois.

(As Geneviève admonishes thus the young messenger, Anne stirs, awakens, and turns with her child in her hands to discover the two speaking. Meanwhile Louis pulls himself from his bed, wraps himself in his robe and comes to the passageway between the bedchamber and the salon where Anne had been resting. He also stands and listens curiously to Geneviève and the messenger)

MESSENGER

Yes, madam. But they both claim to come on urgent matters.

LOUIS XII

What manner of intrusion do you speak against, Geneviève? On whose behalf does the boy come? Hmm?

GENEVIÈVE

'Tis Lord Montauban to see the Queen, and the Cardinal to speak with you, Your Majesty. I told the boy—

LOUIS XII

(cutting her off) I would have news of battle. Bring Monseigneur Amboise to our chambers.

DUCHESS ANNE

Philippe has no doubt good reasons to request an unprepared audience. It is unlike him to forgo ceremony. Have him enter.

MESSENGER

Aye, Your Majesty.

(Geneviève is perplexed but waves the boy on, as he bows to the King and Queen. A moment later, the messenger reappears with both Montauban and Amboise.)

My Lords Amboise and Montauban.

(Messenger steps to the side and bows the head as the two men enter and then, bowing, takes leave of them)

LOUIS XII

Welcome, my fellows. Gaze at our newborn child, our heir.

MONTAUBAN

(Bowing with friendly pleasure in particular to Lady Anne and, smiling, bends to look at the baby in her arms.) Ah, 'tis a girl!

AMBOISE

(bowing, with less enthusiasm towards Lady Anne but polite, preoccupied, obviously, by other matters) What a pity!

(As Amboise says this in disappointment, Lady Anne exchanges with King Louis a look of discontent that reflects distance, worry and slight confusion. She shirks off the Cardinal's unkindly expressed discouragement)

MONTAUBAN

(delighted, bending to extend a finger to the playful baby) Here be our next duchess, my lady.

LOUIS XII

(miffed, correcting him) Here be our next queen!

AMBOISE

A weakly lass, not so, Your Majesty? *(looking at King Louis with concern)* She will need a strong consort – a leader she will not be.

(King Louis notes the discourtesy Amboise is showing and the annoyance he is arousing in Lady Anne by his unkind remarks concerning their newborn daughter)

LOUIS XII

Be seated, my lords. What news of the war, Amboise?

AMBOISE

A victory, sir, complete and unequivocal. We have taken Naples.

MONTAUBAN

(interrupting) Not without considerable cost, Your Majesty, which is my business with you today, my lady. *(turning to Lady Anne, gently, sadly)* The Breton ships you sent in support of the Italian campaign, which formed the bulk of the marine forces, received considerable losses. Several ships went down and many Bretons with them, our finest sailors among them, and many Frenchmen.

AMBOISE

Peasants or nobility?

ANNE

(looking at Amboise with contempt) Does it matter?

MONTAUBAN

(looking away and walking downstage, revealing as well his dislike of Amboise) Commoners, my lord, not of your class.

AMBOISE

Ah well, *(relieved)* 'tis not tragic. And we *are* victorious.

LOUIS XII

But what cost, Amboise? How many lives, Montauban?

MONTAUBAN

(turning to face the King) My lord, I could not count them. At the least, hundreds.

LOUIS XII

(unhappy, pause) How can such slaughter be a victory? *(looking again at Amboise, disillusioned with his judgement but dependent on his sense of realism and diplomacy)* Naples is firmly under your control?

AMBOISE

Aye, my lord, with an even greater treasure behind its ramparts.

(expression of self-satisfaction)

MONTAUBAN

(in concurrent conversation with Queen Anne) There has been deliberate destruction of your ladyship's fleet, Breton vessels. Seven, my lady. Among them, our major vessel, the one you, Lady Anne, rode upon to cross the Mediterranean, protected by its vast breadth and numerous guns.

ANNE

The Cordelière has been destroyed!

MONTAUBAN

By Sforza's cannons and the fire of Borgia's guns. There were a few survivors, but the crew was mostly lost, in the waters.

ANNE

Good God! What condolences do I extend to the Bretons, Louis? How many widows and hungry children are to be consoled by Lord Amboise's declaration that *we*, France, are victorious, that *we* have reaffirmed our national glory and authority in a foreign land? How could we have dragged the Breton people into this personal war of yours, my King?

LOUIS XII

Remember, Anne, you swore political loyalty to France. And also, my lady, among those who died were many, many Frenchmen. I labour no less righteously, my Queen, for French glory than you for Breton dignity. We are of the same race, Anne. *(pause, slightly cynical)* How like your father you have become! François II also spoke to me of Brittany's historical aspiration to remain innocent, pure, non-engaged and untouched by crime and international war. As I said to your father, my lady, Brittany is no less stained by blood than others, than France. *(pause)* But the end is near, Naples having been taken.

AMBOISE

(smiling) I repeat, my lord, there is a particular treasure in our booty, one which you will relish, sir. *(pause)* We have taken Sforza.

LOUIS XII

At last!

AMBOISE

He was attempting to pass by our men as one of the common soldiers, but he was recognised and brought to me. He is in chains, in the courtyard, apart from the others, so you may distinguish him, sir, from your tower.

LOUIS XII

(goes to the centre forestage and looks towards the audience, peering, a broad, vengeful smile comes upon his face). Aye, 'tis he, Sforza, who betrayed Charles and slew so many of my men, mercilessly. Put him in the dungeon, Amboise.

ANNE

My husband Charles showed you mercy. Do not brutalise his enemy.

LOUIS XII

Charles was a merciful man. I am as well when it does not concern an enemy or a traitor to his men. *(pause)* We will see, Anne. For the time, let us talk no more of war and prisoners. *(pause, turning to the two, Montauban and Amboise)* We are glad of your coming, gentle lords. Queen Anne and I will be consulting you on the morrow. We are most glad and bid you good evening.

(Montauban and Amboise rise)

MONTAUBAN

Have cheer, Anne. *(smiling and fondling her daughter's hand)* There is new life for Brittany. *(reaching for and kissing her hand)* A beautiful heir, my lady.

AMBOISE

Aye. *(without enthusiasm, for civility's sake)*

(Both Montauban and Amboise leave, followed by Geneviève. Lights fade)

END OF SCENE V

SCENE VI

(Lights come up, a few minutes after Scene V. Audience sees an intimate dinner in an elegantly furnished salon; a fire in fireplace. A

group of musicians play softly in the background. Geneviève serves wine to the four who rise at the King and Queen's instigation to sit in the parlour. The table where they were seated is upstage centre. The King leads Archduchess Juana (La Loca) of Castile to the divan and Archduke Philippe of Austria leads Queen Anne to a chair.

Geneviève comes in, carrying a pitcher of wine from which she has just poured. Absentmindedly, she happens to notice the audience as she moves downstage left. The two couples are in indiscernible, almost silent discussion while Geneviève addresses the audience. Geneviève sighs at her work, puts the pitcher of wine down on a table. She goes to the fireplace and waves her apron to fan it and brings the heat towards her)

GENEVIÈVE

Good evening. It is now December 1502, some years later. *(Geneviève continues to fan the fire and enjoys the heat while she is speaking)* We are at the King's castle in Blois. It is a very special occasion, you see. With my Lady Anne is, of course, the King and the Archduke Philippe le Beau with his young wife, Princess Juana of

Castile, soon to be called Juana La Loca. La Infanta Lady Juana is the daughter of Isabella of Castile and Ferdinand of Aragon. Very powerful. The monarchs who are uniting Spain. After the death of her brothers, Princess Juana will inherit the entire Kingdom of Castile. Look at the adoration she bears her handsome husband Philippe le Beau. He is the son of the Austrian Emperor. It is a sensible marriage, preparing a legacy of vast combinations of empires to be controlled by their heir. All of the Hapsburg Empire, Spain, the Netherlands and what will later become the French province of Franche-Comté. A tremendous empire to be inherited by the first-born son of Juana and Philippe le Beau. And indeed, a year and eight months before this royal visit, Juana gave birth to the future Emperor, Charles. Why, he is to become the powerful monarch of his time, Charles V.

QUEEN ANNE

(For the last minute or two Duchess Anne has been watching Geneviève whom she now approaches) But do they *(gesturing to the audience)* understand why the King and myself are entertaining

Princess Juana and Archduke Philippe; what the purpose is of their visit and this scene?

GENEVIÈVE

Well, I—

QUEEN ANNE

(interrupting) Simply put, we, the French, are battling the Austrian and the Spanish for possession of much of Italy, particularly the duchies of Milan and Naples. What better resolution than to marry our little Claude to the future emperor! And what more glorious marriage could be possible for our daughter!

(King Louis looks up at this point from his conversation with Juana and Philippe and gazes at Queen Anne, moved, yet uncertain)

What better way to protect Brittany and my daughter's inherited role as sovereign ruler of the Bretons? That is why we dine together this evening. That is why the Archduke and the Archduchess will stay in Blois for a week as they pass from the Netherlands to Aragon.

(Anne sees Claude come to her, picks her up and holds her. She doesn't notice that Claude has wandered in with Louise de Savoie and her son François who approach arrogantly and curiously from the right downstage along an extended curtain)

Ah, my lovely!

(Anne begins to affectionately lead Princess Claude to meet the company, when Louise de Savoie and François are noticed behind them by Louis, as he looks up with pleasure. Meanwhile the King has wandered over to the right downstage, to address the audience in confidence as Queen Anne speaks)

LOUIS XII

It is unfortunate, but this very year I made a secret agreement that Claude would marry no one but my adopted ward, François of Angoulême. No one knows of this, not even my Brett, Queen Anne, that is. There was no real choice but at least France gains an alliance and friends, that is until the end of our Italian expedition. And neither Brittany nor France will be an appendage to the Austrians; at least, until then, neither the Austrians nor the Spaniards will oppose me. *(louder)* Eh, Brett, look what company attends.

(Queen Anne, puzzled, turns around and, upon seeing Louise de Savoie, her expression changes to polite displeasure. Savoie meets her look with equal resentment. Although Savoie does not succeed in attempting to hide her curiosity, she feigns successfully pleasure, sweetness and courtesy. Meanwhile Princess Juana, not yet noticing Savoie and François, watches little Princess Claude being led or carried into the room by Queen Anne)

JUANA

Ah, es guerida. Buenos noches, mi preciosa. A most beautiful child, Lady Anne.

QUEEN ANNE

Muchas gracias, mi empresa, tiene cuatro años y es muy timida con la gente.

JUANA

Y la princessa Renée?

QUEEN ANNE

Dorma. Our youngest is not present. She is only two, and has not yet the wide-eyed stamina of Princess Claude.

(Draws Claude to her. Princess Claude appears fascinated by the beautiful Spanish Empress and attracted also to the medallion necklace around her neck. The Empress gathers the child in her arms and places her nearby)

JUANA

Look, Philippe, she is as I was at her age. How she resembles me!

PHILIPPE

The Princess Claude is as beautiful but far more spirited, I would say. *(silence and hurt shown by Juana. Philippe is a bit drunk.)* I would hope the comparison goes no further. She grows to womanhood in a humane, tolerant court. Whereas you, mi guerida, grew up by the side of Queen Isabella and the lugubrious, solemn court of the Inquisition. *(Drinks and addresses them all)* Nay, fear not, there the likeness stops.

(Juana regains her composure. Queen Anne and King Louis glance at each other, embarrassed, sensitive to Juana's humiliation; at this moment the King calls to Lady Savoie to present herself and her son)

LOUIS XII

Ah, Lady Louise! Have you dined? Come, join our evening company!

(the King gestures to Lady Savoie to present herself and her son. As Savoie approaches, she loosens the hand of her son François which she has been holding. François, here, is a young boy of sixteen, eager, quick, and ambitious)

QUEEN ANNE

(politely) May I present to Your Highnesses the Emperor and Empress of Austria, Lady Louise de Savoie, Duchess of Angoulême, and young François d'Angoulême, the ward of my husband, His Majesty.

LADY SAVOIE

I am honoured.

(She presses François's arm as she curtseys so that François is encouraged to bow to the Archduke and Archduchess who nod and smile in acknowledgement)

LOUIS XII

(Coming forward to slap young François on the shoulder) Young François is the son I have not had.

(Duchess Anne looks down. Lady Savoie triumphantly and unkindly looks at her and enjoys her discomfort)

He has not taken his eyes off you, sir, since your arrival in Blois. Did you not see this excited young lad in the party that met your cavalcade?

(Louis addresses François) Well, François, already tantalised, already envious of grandeur and power? *(embarrassment and silence from others. Louis looks reflectively at him)* He wishes to be my successor. Well, my boy, not tonight.

(Group of men separates from women, as everyone laughs)

PHILIPPE

(Laughs) Ambition makes a great man strong, provided he comprehends his passions. Do you, François?

FRANÇOIS

Passions, sir?

PHILIPPE

(in German) You are not yet a man but you know what passion is. *(To King Louis)* As your vassal, my King, I will not precede you in offering your ward this vital knowledge. *(laughs)*

LOUISE DE SAVOIE

(Preparing to leave) We do bid Your Majesties good night and beg you do excuse this impulsive intrusion. François wished so to meet Your Highness, and Princess Claude wished to bid her mother good evening. The children often play together, you see. As cousins, they are most attached. *(disbelieving silence)* Come François, kiss your cousin good night.

(François has to be led forcefully by Savoie to kiss Claude and finds the embrace upsetting)

PHILIPPE

(joking as François passes) One learns to nourish and condone one's passion if that is one's destiny. *(firmly taking the boy's arm, looking at him with meaning)* In this case, my boy, it is not yours. It is mine.

FRANÇOIS

(Bravely) We shall see, my lord.

(Everyone but Louis stiffens from shock and outrage at François's impertinent manner. Less shocked than the others, Louis approaches the boy, discerning yet sceptical)

PHILIPPE

Why, you impudent child! *(He speaks with quiet, controlled anger. He laughs viciously, then notices François's fascination with Louis's sword)* François has visions, my amiable king – see how he eyes our crowns and swords. I should not turn my back on him.

LOUIS XII

(smiling, amiably also) I do not.

PHILIPPE

Is his swordsman's skill as strong as his tongue?

LOUIS XII

Ah yes, I have exercised him myself for nearly six years.

PHILIPPE

(Takes his sword from his sheath) I would be sure!

LOUIS XII

This is a mission of peace and rapprochement in which we are engaged, Philippe, not a Roman execution. We must remember the truce signed with your father, Maximilian of Austria. The whole of Europe, thank God, is at peace. France and Austria need not battle until war is inevitable. And you, sir, *(pause)* need not fight a boy. It diminishes you.

(François, meanwhile, has grabbed a guard's sword and races to challenge Philippe. Louis, seeing this, calmly unsheathes his own sword and uses it to cut in front of François, stopping him.)

François! *(pause)* These are not the manners of a gentleman, much less a king before combat. *(observing François's and Philippe's determination)* Very well. You shall meet each other. Let us call it an 'exercise'.

(The women protest. But Louis is firm in his decision to arbitrate) Nay, 'tis an 'exercise' and they must meet each other.

(Lights fade for a moment. Stage is in darkness. Then lights come up again. The characters wear capes, as they appear to be outside. One sees only the figures, no scenery. Everyone is in nearly the exact position from moments prior)

LOUIS XII

My dear Majesty, do you challenge François d'Angoulême?

PHILIPPE

Aye! *(With anticipation, waving his sword)*

LOUIS XII

(Comically; puzzled, as he is playing by the rules, following the etiquette of a duel) Then *do* so, sir.

PHILIPPE

(Philippe wakes as if from a dream and hands him his glove, brushing it slightly across François's nose beforehand) Voilà!

LOUIS XII

Très bien. Vos places, messieurs! *(Each backs away a few steps)* Salutation. Rapprochement. *(The men come together, crossing swords, following a mutual bow)* Et, en garde!

(Louis walks downstage left as the men battle intensely; clearly he wishes to know if François can meet Philippe in combat successfully; clearly the victor of this duel will be, in his eyes, the next King of France. After a minute of combat culminating in matched swords beating each other, Louis places his sword to separate them and start them again)

LOUIS XII

Rapprochement. En garde!

(As François and Philippe battle, their movements become quicker and more intense. At the same time, Louise de Savoie follows her son's movements determinedly. She moves with him and behind him with discreet distance. Juana la Loca slowly loses control and cries out each moment Philippe seems in danger. Eventually Queen Anne goes over to calm Empress Juana, on the verge of hysteria. Philippe, though courteous and dashing in manner, disregards completely the distress of his young wife and finally says)

PHILIPPE

Leave me, madame. Retire to your chambers if you find this distasteful.

QUEEN ANNE

I believe, sir, the Empress Juana fears that, despite your obvious superiority and prowess, *(this angers Savoie and François)* she fears an injury.

PHILIPPE

(laughing ironically) How unlike her! The Spaniards burn the flesh of living disbelievers and yet they refuse the challenge of an amusing spectacle.

(Juana is struck to the heart by this last blow. Crushed and disorientated, she has begun to be led offstage by Geneviève whom Queen Anne had signalled to assist her. Juana stops and continues to

watch the duel. Princess Claude, seeing François in danger, goes to him, cries and pulls on his arm)

FRANÇOIS

(Annoyed) Let us alone! *(pause)* Go away!

(Queen Anne is shocked by the violence of the scene, by the insensitivity of Philippe and François, and by the mirroring of identities in Claude and Juana as well as in Philippe and François. Anne shares a look of embarrassment and concern with Louis; she goes to her daughter, holds her closer to her. Everyone is shaken by the increasing violence and rage of young François whose movements and emotions are shadowed and imitated by Louise de Savoie. As the sword fight continues, Queen Anne stares with alarm at François and Philippe. She then watches intensely Claude and Juana and their mutually anguished reactions. Queen Anne motions to Geneviève and, with her help, they finally lead Juana and Claude offstage, supposedly to their chambers. Queen Anne returns to speak briefly to Louis)

QUEEN ANNE

Louis?

LOUIS XII

Hmm?

QUEEN ANNE

The close resemblance between Philippe and François. Claude mirrors the possible neglect and hysteria of she who already is called Juana La Loca. And Louise. *(gazing at her)* She reminds me of Juana's mother, Queen Isabella, who protects with such unscrupulous terrorism the legacy of her children. *(pauses to reflect)* I would be afraid for Claude were she ever to marry this boy. He has the cruel strength and ambition of his mother and would crush our daughter, as Philippe has crushed Juana. If Claude were to marry the grandson of the Emperor, the son of Juana and Philippe, at least Brittany would be protected by enormous power and rank. And Claude would not be married to a cruel, vicious pretender to power. Hmmph, already he beds the maids of magistrates and the daughters of our barons.

LOUIS XII

And France?

QUEEN ANNE

France would remain sovereign, under Claude and young Charles. We have the Emperor's written agreement. It is *Brittany* which would be engulfed and lost should the new king be under the thumb of Savoie. We both know this.

LOUIS XII

Aye!

(Wearily, he gets up, seeing no definite victor. As he prepares to call an end to the duel, Philippe trips, falls and begins quickly to rise. As he does so, François, tempted, bursts towards him, ready to pierce him in the back of the neck. Louis, having seen François's intention,

surges forward and swings his own sword to knock François's weapon from his hand, scratching François's hand with his sword. François drops his sword in pain and cries out; Louis remains where he had positioned himself for the blow, while Louise hurries forward to see to François's injury. Anne steps forward halfway between Louis and Philippe, desiring to assist Philippe. Savoie looks up angrily at Louis whereas Louis returns her gaze with intensity. Then Louis and Anne look at each other, mutually fully comprehending the dangerous character of François. Without taking his eyes off Queen Anne, King Louis speaks)*

Relinquish your weapons, gentlemen, there will be no resolution of this matter this evening.

(The fighting thus ends and Philippe puts his hand on François's shoulder)

PHILIPPE

'Twas a test, my boy *(pause)* which you failed.

(François jerks away angrily and starts to move offstage, his mother hovering over him.) Till another time, my young adversary! *(laughs)* Most considerate, Your Majesty, to have flung aside the sword of your protégé. My son, you see, will make a better husband for your Claude. Good evening, my lady, Your Majesty.

LOUIS XII

Good evening *(pause)* Philippe. *(Philippe stops, midway towards offstage followed by valets)* Was your life worth the gamble, to test young François?

PHILIPPE

Aye, my king. Now you know the worth of us both, and I the measure of you, sir. *(bows and moves offstage)*

(Queen Anne and King Louis remain on stage as the lights fade but focus intensely upon them. Queen Anne pulls her cape tightly around

her as Louis stands perpendicular with a gaze offstage, at an angle to the audience, who sees mostly his back)

QUEEN ANNE

Promise me, Louis. Claude shall not pine away in neglect and humiliation. *(turning to him)* Promise me that your successor, the next King of France, will not be young François. Promise me that our daughter will marry an emperor's heir who would protect France, not an ambitious young aristocrat who might well crush the will of our child and of Brittany. Promise me, Louis. *(This last sentence said quietly. Anne exits)*

LOUIS XII

Who indeed is the better husband? A coward, or a son of tyrants?

(lights fade)

END OF SCENE VI

SCENE VII

AMBOISE

(Amboise, centre upstage. King Louis right downstage. Geneviève enters and begins to sweep among, around and in front of them.)

The Blois treaty document, sir, needs your signature.

LOUIS XII

Aye, proceed, Cardinal.

AMBOISE

First, the treaty reads: 'There shall be an indissoluble alliance between Maximilian, Emperor of the Holy Roman Empire, Louis XII Sovereign of France and Philippe, Archduke of Austria and Ruler of the Netherlands, an indissoluble alliance which makes the three, one united soul in three bodies. This will constitute the investiture within three months of the Dukedom of Milan for Louis XII and his male descendants or, in the absence of these latter, Charles de

Luxembourg, heir to the Empire, and Princesse Claude, heir to the throne of France.'

LOUIS XII

Aye!

AMBOISE

The treaty further reads. . .

(The discussion between the two men continues, inaudibly. To the left we see a darkened prison dungeon with stairs at the back of the stage and a window to the right A guard stands backstage towards the left. A prisoner chained to the wall in rags, facing the wall, is being whipped by guards. Down the passage stairway in the back comes a servant with a lantern, leading a figure in a cape. As the figure descends, the audience recognises the features of Queen Anne who flings back the hood of her cape. The guards, recognising her, kneel, stammer, "Your Majesty," and stand aside)

QUEEN ANNE

This is the man whose cries haunt the evenings and the days. What confession do you seek from him with your beatings?

GUARD

None, my lady. It is his name and his crime which he will not recant, for which King Louis demands his punishment.

QUEEN ANNE

(bending down to the prisoner to discover his identity) The man is bloody and nearly dead. Who could it be to merit such unusual punishment?

GUARD

This, my lady, is Duke Ludovico Sforza.

(As the guard pronounces his name, he turns him and we see Sforza's maddened, weakened bloody face as he faces Queen Anne.)

QUEEN ANNE

(Stunned by the name) Sforza! He who led Charles into battle and abandoned him there. Sforza – who betrayed both my husbands and sent his armies to kill them, slaying hundreds.

(She suddenly strikes across his face, hard and brutally with the guard's whip. After hitting Sforza she drops the whip, stunned and fearful of her own violence) Let him not be a martyr. Beat him no more. Feed and cleanse him. *(with a show of moral repugnance)* Punish him with solitude and keep him far from my sight.

(Queen Anne dons her hood and moves upstage quickly, followed by her servant who carries the lantern. Lights fade on this part of the stage. We see again only Amboise and the King who have just finished reviewing the clauses of the Blois Treaties which provide mainly for the marriage of Claude, their daughter and Charles of Luxembourg, grandson of the Emperor Maximilian and son of Philippe le Beau and Juana La Loca. Charles is the heir to both the Empire and the newly united Iberian peninsula)

LOUIS XII

Yea, Brett, my lady, I will accept the terms of the Treaty and the marriage of our Claude to the Emperor's heir, Charles of Luxembourg. But know this, I do so because it would give France political advantage. It will protect French domains in Italy and it would give us Austrian protection against the League of Italian States, against the ambitious plotting of Julian, the Pope, who used his papal authority to draw me into war against Venice; now he abandons us and begins to turn our neighbours against us. Ha! *(pause)* Do you remember, Brett, how he blessed us when we gave our soldiers and arms to another crusade in the Holy Land, to oust the Turkish infidels, to extend Vatican imperialism over Venice, Florence and Naples? How he *lured* us with his self-righteous prayers and calls for divine justice! Young Machiavelli warned me against him, in this very chamber – remember, Amboise? Have you read the work in which he analyses, as an example of the statesman's classic political errors, my dealings with Pope Julian? *(intensely)* Yea, this treaty will solidify our alliance with the Emperor who will rule Spain, Holland and Austria. France would be protected from the ambitions of other princes.

Know, Brett, that I sign, that I accept this idealistic agreement in the hope that it may be applied. And, in doing so, you must know that, in judging its goals and its application, *(pause) I do so for France.* I agree to give my daughter to the Emperor's grandson, the future Charles V, but *not* for Brittany, and, though I love her as much as I adore her mother *(pause)* I do *this not* for *Claude.* I do *this* for France. *(Determined)* The moment it becomes clear that the Treaty binds us, not others, the moment I see France threatened, I will not feel further bound by these Blois agreements.

QUEEN ANNE

(slowly regaining her composure following her visit to the dungeon) Aye, *(pause, then softly, but firmly)* but we have no choice: the Pope threatened you, Louis, with excommunication; he holds in his hands the Catholic world. He is, for better or worse, the paramount spiritual authority on earth.

LOUIS XII

He is *not* my master, madam. Nor does he command the power you impute to him.

QUEEN ANNE

His predecessor sanctified our right to marry. In our minds we are in the Catholic dominion of papal authority, my lord. Yea, I urged you to join him in the Crusade; I gave Brittany's navy, her finest men and ships to assist France's military expeditions. But I would that I had wielded the power to keep you out of Italy. It has obsessed you no less than your cousin, Charles. *(going to him)* You have justly earned, Louis, the title Father of the People as you have fathered justice and humanity in your own land. Why do you father chaos and war elsewhere with uselessly obstinate claims of heretical right? Why do you demean yourself by martyring our enemy? *(Louis looks at her, uncomprehending)* Sforza is dying, my love. I stopped your guards from beating him to death, not knowing who he was. Then, having discovered his identity, I struck him with all my strength and *(shocked at herself*) by heaven I would have killed him. *(pause)* But I've stopped the beatings – he will be fed and bathed but, mark you, Louis, send him far from my sight. I felt myself relive poor Chancellor Chauvin's death and Landais's merciless hanging. Now we are the monarchs to be judged, my King – there is no pity even for benevolent tyrants such as we – when, on the day of reckoning, God denies our divine right to rule and sends us to hell and back for our acts of glory and revenge.

LOUIS XII

Sforza's fate is of little interest to me and although I gave no order that he be beaten, I care not. But it shall be as you wish, my lady: he shall be removed to another prison, fed and cleansed and left to suffer no greater physical torture than that of lonely solitude. But you, Brett, as you carry further the burdens of royal conscience, know this. *(pause)* I am a statesman, a king, and as such, I do not apologise for my practical immorality. Had I not pursued our rights to our dominions in Italy I, like so many others, would have been perceived as weak – not humane, not just, not honourable – but weak. And weakness in a king, my lady Anne, is the most costly of reputations. Spain, Austria, England were all prepared to pounce upon our foreign territories. And after seizing them with no resistance from willing, humane, compassionate King Louis, France was the next intended victim. This is not mere supposition, Brett, for we have proof – letters and spies who informed us well. Would you have done any less to defend the Bretons? *(pause)* No, I fancy not. But fear not. I have given my word. I agree to our Blois Treaties and Claude's marriage, praying as you do, Brett, that the Emperor honours his word and written hand. *(pause)* In the meantime, the Parisians expect you, Brett, to enter their city for the first time, for your coronation as my Queen.

(Louis comes to Anne, holds her, pressing her close to him and kissing her neck) Come to bed, my lady. *(pause)* I am tired.

ANNE

(vacant-eyed, disturbed) Nay, not this evening, Louis.

(attempts to move away)

LOUIS XII

(holding her, his arms the length of her own) **Anne!** Brett! Come, this night I would be with no one else.

(Anne's back is to Louis who presses her to him. As she throws back her head upon his shoulder, scene closes. Lights on Amboise, Louis and Anne fade)

END OF SCENE VII

SCENE VIII

(Lights on, a play is in progress. We see the characters performing. Among the people sitting in audience are Queen Anne and King Louis. Dialogue of comic play (25); laughter, including that of Queen and King. François sits sullenly with Louise de Savoie. Geneviève serves liquid refreshment. As she moves off towards downstage centre she puts on one of the costumes and goes on the play stage as a character and says a few lines. We hear laughter. She then returns offstage the imagined play but still on stage in our actual

drama. She changes masks and costumes and goes again to take on another role. This role is a serious one. Again she changes to another costume and mask offstage the imagined play. She returns onstage and again plays a role. We hear laughter again. Coming out of the play)

GENEVIÈVE

'Tis a task to play so many roles.

(As Geneviève speaks, Claude appears and approaches her. Claude is now the same age as her mother when she played the same scene with Geneviève)

CLAUDE

Geneviève, whom will I marry?

GENEVIÈVE

Ah, go to bed, girl, the play's too long for you to fret about its ending.

CLAUDE

Mother says I'll be an empress soon. Father shakes his head and spends long hours with François, teaching him the art of government.

GENEVIÈVE

(She goes on to play another role and comes back, exhausted)

Child, you're young and strong and loving. *(lifting her up as she had her mother years ago)* You'll be a queen, part of history. *(lowers her down; then mischievous)* Whom do you fancy? Go to bed, child, the play is over.

(Geneviève plays another role and goes offstage with Claude, returns and carries with her a pitcher.

Cardinal Amboise whispers news in the King's ear. King Louis, upon reflecting, turns to Anne amidst the laughing and gazes at her as she laughs also at the play. After this considerable pause, he speaks to her)

LOUIS XII

My lady, the Emperor has allied with the Pope and declares war on France. *(pause)* I shall arrange the marriage contract ceremony between Claude and the Duke François of Angoulême. *(another pause)* The Blois Treaties are now invalid. *(He watches Anne's sudden stillness; Geneviève is between them)*

QUEEN ANNE

(pause, far from reality) I shall be off, soon, to Brittany, to inspect the tomb of my father. There are sanctuaries, roads, that await my inspection and Parliament meets soon in Rennes. I think I will lead a pilgrimage next year. They are harvesting a crop of sugar beet and cherries. I must be there, with the Bretons.

LOUIS XII

(gently) Aye, Brett.

(The laughter continues as Geneviève goes to play another role. King Louis stares at Duchess Anne. Both of them are still, amidst the laughter. Lights fade)

END OF SCENE VIII

SCENE IX

(Louis is in the position of the first scene. He gazes ahead into space, obviously absorbing the presence and absence of Duchess Anne. He looks tired and older, as in the first scene of the play)

LOUIS XII

I had not intended, Brett, to be alone. I had hoped you would outlive me.

(Voices are heard. We see François and Louise come on stage. They do not see Louis and are in the corner of downstage right)

FRANÇOIS

When the old man dies, France will have its first Renaissance King. I will win in Italy where my predecessors lost, and Brittany will become an integral part of France.

LOUISE

Have you seen young Mary – the English Princess King Louis weds tomorrow? I say, she seems to fancy you, François. And you, her – might it be?

FRANÇOIS

Aye, but I'm told her true love is an English knight who accompanies her party, that Mary cuckolds old King Louis before and after they are wed. *(laughing with his mother)* Ah, Mother, he will not long outlive Duchess Anne, with a passionate bride to satisfy.

(Discussion between Savoie and François becomes inaudible as we see Philippe Montauban enter and approach the King)

LOUIS XII

Ah, Montauban, my friend. *(clasps his hands earnestly)* I am grateful for your presence.

MONTAUBAN

(Bowing; much older, tired, yet of humble, simple demeanour) With all respect, Your Majesty, I served Lady Anne until the last with honour, for she was the *last* true *duchess* of Brittany; and, in my eyes, the most legitimate. *(pause)* I have done as you asked, Your Majesty: the small ermine presented to Duchess Anne at the coronation as the symbol of the royal ducal arms of Brittany has been given to Claude. I found as well verses Lady Anne had treasured, given to her by her court poet Marot upon the occasion of the birth of her firstborn, the

first heir who did not live, Charles Orlando. I gave those as well to little Claude, my lord.

(King Louis and Montauban watch Claude enter with the ermine over her shoulder, caressing it and carrying an unrolled parchment. She reads the poem written years ago by Clément Marot for Duchess Anne's heir. Montauban, moved, bids adieu to King Louis in a broken voice)

My lord.

(King Louis inclines the head and continues to listen with pleasure, as if he were hearing again Queen Anne's voice as a young woman. Suddenly François approaches Claude, laughs, snatches the paper from her and tears it apart)

FRANÇOIS

Ha! Ha! What sentimental trappings of Duchess Anne, to no purpose. And you, my lady, *(the last few words said sarcastically as François bows mockingly)* will not need to read when I am king.

You'll be too occupied with the bearing of my heirs and the caring of my bastards.

(Both he and Louise de Savoie laugh cruelly. François sees the ermine on Claude's frightened arm) What's this? A pet of Duchess Anne's? I'll have no vestige of Brittany's rebellion in my court.

(King Louis had risen angrily as François tore the parchment on which Anne's poem was written. During François's action, described above, Louis makes his way towards François and his mother and unsheathes his sword. As François begins to threaten the ermine, Louis bursts forward angrily, wields his sword and, as in the previous scene, knocks François's sword from his hand, again injuring him. François reacts, as before, with angry pain as he and his mother huddle together in surprise)

LOUIS XII

You will not dispose of a legacy, you pathetic bully. How dare you threaten the liberty and mind of my child, who bears more depth and honesty than you or your mother could ever know? You may insult me, miscreant; you may delight in my ageing, futile intercourse; but *do not dare* to touch, to breathe, do not hope to live should you stain Anne of Brittany's memory with your cowardly, cruel insults. And you, *(turning to speak to Louise de Savoie)* madam, do not imagine for a moment that I have not divined your role in the fate of the innocent sons of Charles and Anne. *(looks at François with pity)* You are not fit to be a king, boy! Go! Leave us! Before I denounce you both!

(as they leave) Good God, forgive me for sparing the bastard's life, for making him a king. *(pause. Change to calmer state)* As you have heard, Brett, Brittany is lost. *(pause)* I had hoped to conceive a more worthy heir, with young Mary. . . but *(smiling sadly)*, my love, my time is past, as is my gift for procreation. *(pause)* Oh, how still the air is. *(pause)* Yes, I still have passions and desire and will think of nothing else this evening before I marry and love and drink – and die. Louis XII, I have been. A duke fighting for Brittany. A king fighting for France. *(pause)* Sweet Brett. How I long for your peace!

(He stirs, as Geneviève comes in sweeping, wiping her brow. He returns to his reflecting and sits, staring at nothing)

GENEVIÈVE

Well, that be our drama for this evening. Good night to you, kind ladies and gentlemen.

(continues sweeping until lights fade.

As play ends and curtains close, audience hears performance of 'En amours n'a si non bien'.) (26)

Notes

1. 'En amours n'a si non bien': musical composition of the fifteenth century, author unknown.
2. 'Ne je ne dors': by Guillaume Dufay (1474).
3. 'Greensleeves': English late-medieval verse and melody.
4. Old Breton ballad.
5. Ovid: *L'Art d'Aimer, Les Amours*: translated from the French edition; Editions Athena, Paris; 1948
6. Ovid: *Les Tristes*; livre IV: pp.115-7; translated from the French version; Société d'édition, les Belles Lettres, Paris; 1938.
7. Ibid.
8. Jehan Meschinot, troubadour of fifteenth-century France: *Les Lunettes des Princes*; Librairie des Bibliophiles, Paris; 1890.
9. 'Mi ut re ut': musical composition of the late fifteenth century.
10. Vivaldi: Concerto in B Minor for two violins, strings and basso continuo.
11. 'Le Petit Pont': *Chansons et textes du Vieux Brest*: Yverdalgue.
12. Ibid.
13. 'Le Diable noir': *Chansons et textes du Vieux Brest*: Yverdalgue; melody combined with verse by Charles d'Orléans in the early fifteenth century.
14. 'En amours n'a si non bien'. *(see note 1)*
15. melody from 'Le Diable noir'. *(see note 13)*
16. 'Mi ut re ut'. *(see note 9)*

17. 'Chant de mal et de vertu' (Song of evil and of virtue): poem by Clément Marot of sixteenth-century France; part of poem translated into English by author, *Anthologie de la poésie française*; p.60; Librairie de Nantes, Paris; 1929.
18. 'Greensleeves' *(see note 3)* or Concerto in B Minor by Vivaldi. *(see note 10)*
19. Ariosto, Ludovico: *Orlando Furioso*; pp.330 & 346; Flammarion, Paris; 1982.
20. Ibid.
21. Ibid.
22. Old Breton ballad.
23. Ovid: *L'Art d'Aimer*. *(see note 5)*
24. 'Mi ut re ut'.
25. To be drawn from either of the following comedies: 'Maître Mimin étudiant' or 'Les Gens Nouveaux': *Farces du Moyen Age*; Flammarion; 1984.
26. 'En amours n'a si non bien'. *(see note 1)*